DANGEROUS QUESTIONS

Catherine had what she wanted—a proposal from the irreproachable Earl of Strickland. Why then did she tremble when Stephen Archibald asked "Do you love him?"

And why did she answer "N-no"?

"You are certain?" There was no question about it this time. His breath was warm and moist against her ear, causing an involuntary shiver. What was he doing to her? Why did she not simply push him away?

"Y-yes, I am certain," she heard herself saying, as his hand reached up to her neck and began untying the ribbon of her bonnet. The soft touch of his fingers upon her throat was making it almost impossible to breathe.

His lips came down on hers. They were unexpectedly soft and warm from the sun when they touched hers, moving slowly in a way she could never have imagined, tasting, exploring, tantalizing, as her mouth opened under his, and became more insistent.

And she could only ask herself what was she doing, even as her heart beat out the answer she could not deny. . . .

A
Garden
Folly

by
Candice Hern

A SIGNET BOOK

SIGNET
Published by the Penguin Group
Penguin Books USA Inc., 375 Hudson Street,
New York, New York 10014, U.S.A.
Penguin Books Ltd, 27 Wrights Lane,
London W8 5TZ, England
Penguin Books Australia Ltd,
Ringwood, Victoria, Australia
Penguin Books Canada Ltd, 10 Alcorn Avenue,
Toronto, Ontario, Canada M4V 3B2
Penguin Books (N.Z.) Ltd, 182–190 Wairau Road,
Auckland 10, New Zealand

Penguin Books Ltd, Registered Offices:
Harmondsworth, Middlesex, England

First published by Signet, an imprint of Dutton Signet,
a division of Penguin Books USA Inc.

First Printing, Jauuary, 1997
10 9 8 7 6 5 4 3 2 1

To Mom and Pop
who taught me everything I know
about romance.
This one's for you.

Chapter 1

"How curious."

At the sound of her sister's voice, Catherine Forsythe looked up from the red leather account book, grateful for any distraction from the depressing figures before her. She had reached her wit's end. She did not have a single idea how they were to scrape up the money to get them through the end of the month. She absently pushed aside a stray wisp of ash blond hair with the end of her quill and regarded her sister.

Two years Catherine's senior at two-and-twenty, Susannah stood staring out the window overlooking the street below. The late-morning sun spilled in through the paned glass and transformed her pale yellow curls into spun gold. Catherine smiled at the vision her beautiful sister made. Susannah looked for all the world like a northern Renaissance angel plucked from heaven and incongruously placed in a shabby Chelsea sitting room.

Surely all that beauty could be put to good use, somehow. If only the right opportunity would present itself!

"What is it, Susannah?" Catherine asked. "What is so curious?"

"A carriage has pulled up just outside," her sister replied without turning her attention from the window. "And a liveried footman is even now coming up our walk."

"A liveried footman? In this part of Chelsea?" Catherine laughed. "Unlikely. Put on your spectacles, Sukey. It cannot be a liveried footman and whoever it is certainly is not coming to *our* house." At least she hoped he was not. They never had visitors. There were only three chairs left in the sitting room, and those rather plain and worn. The rest of the good furniture had been sold off bit by bit to keep food on the table. And tea was carefully rationed. If there was indeed an uninvited visitor, surely he would not expect tea.

"But I *am* wearing my spectacles," Susannah said as she turned toward the room. "See?"

Catherine bit back a smile as her sister tapped the wire frames for emphasis and widened her blue eyes, already made huge behind the slight magnification of the corrective lenses.

"I can see quite clearly," Susannah continued, "and I tell you there is a footman at our door."

Her words were followed by the sound of the knocker below. "Good heavens!" Catherine cried as she rose from the tiny scarred oak writing desk and joined her sister at the window. True enough, there stood an unmarked but obviously fine black carriage—not a hackney, surely—attached to a pair of glossy chestnuts. The elegant animals danced skittishly while held by a liveried coachman.

Susannah smiled in triumph. "See! I *told* you."

"Yes, you were right. But who in the world can it be?" Catherine turned toward the third occupant of the tiny sitting room. Aunt Hetty had not looked up from her darning, her concentration fixed on mending the toe of a black stocking. Auburn curls sprinkled with silver escaped from the confines of her plain cotton cap. "Aunt Hetty?" Catherine asked. "Are you expecting anyone? You did not mention it."

The older woman looked up. "What's that, dear? Did you say something?"

Catherine was never quite sure if her aunt was hard of hearing or simply oblivious. What with Susannah's general lack of sense, it was a wonder the three of them managed at all. Thank heavens Catherine knew how to use her head or there was no telling what might become of them.

"A footman has come," Susannah said to her aunt in an excited voice. "In a carriage!"

"But he is leaving now," Catherine said as she watched the bewigged young man in splendid blue-and-silver livery climb into the carriage. The coachman jumped back upon his perch and the carriage was on its way. "It must have been a mistake. Wrong house or some such thing." She watched as the carriage disappeared down Flood Street. "Wrong neighborhood, I should think," she added in an undertone.

"He's *gone*?" Susannah nudged her sister aside and peered out the window. "Oh." She drew out the syllable in a long, disappointed sigh. She continued to gaze down the street, as if the carriage might return after all.

Catherine gave her sister's shoulders an affectionate squeeze and returned to the writing desk. She was tempted to heave a sigh of her own. She was not sure if she was glad to have no visitor to worry about, or if she was disappointed by the prospect of relief from the boredom of a summer in Town. For a moment, just for a moment, she had begun to ponder the possibilities of a footman at their door. Somehow she was sure she could have used him to advantage in her plan of recovery. Footmen, after all, were generally employed by people of means.

Catherine had bent her head to resume her fruitless study of their accounts when the sitting room door opened. MacDougal, their single loyal retainer, entered the room and cleared his throat.

"This just arrived by special messenger," he said, a slight burr coloring his words. "For you, ma'am."

A tall, spare man of indeterminate age, MacDougal held out a small silver tray upon which lay a creamy vellum envelope, and offered it to Aunt Hetty. Where on earth had he found a silver tray? Catherine was certain they no longer owned one. She quickly rose once again from the desk and went to MacDougal, determined to examine the tray, when her eyes noted an escutcheoned crest on the thick envelope. Ignoring the tray for the moment, she grabbed up the envelope before her aunt could retrieve it.

"Good heavens, Aunt Hetty, this looks important," she said, caressing the fine vellum between her fingers. She turned it over to discover a red wax seal with two facing lions. She wished she knew more about coats of arms—which families were the lions, the bears, the dragons, that sort of thing. Running a finger over the wax, her mind raced with notions of what important personage might be writing to her penniless aunt. And why. "Now, who do you suppose . . ."

"Perhaps if you would but let me open it, my dear," Aunt Hetty said, her amused tone interrupting the fanciful train of Catherine's thoughts, "we could all learn who has sent it."

"Oh!" Catherine realized that three pairs of eyes had been turned to her. "Oh, of course. How silly of me." She returned the envelope to the tray held out by MacDougal and stood back as he offered it, once again, to Aunt Hetty. Catherine did not miss the twinkle in his dark eyes or the slight twitch at the corners of his mouth as MacDougal bowed and proceeded to quit the room. When he reached the door, he paused and turned.

"Excuse me, ma'am," he said to Aunt Hetty before

she could so much as break the seal on the fine vellum. "I thought ye might like to know that I've come in the way of leg o' mutton. I was wonderin' if ye might be wantin' a bit of it fer supper tonight?"

"A leg of mutton?" Aunt Hetty's eyes grew wide with astonishment.

They had been living on little more than bread and cheese and onions for so many weeks now, that the mere mention of meat caused Catherine's mouth to water. "How on earth did you just happen to come by a leg of mutton, MacDougal?" she asked, her eyes narrowing at the wily retainer. "It did not just happen to fall off the back of a butcher's wagon, I trust?"

MacDougal grinned. "Nae, nae. I ha' it on quite legitimate terms, Miss Catherine. Y' see, me cousin's husband's sister's girl works over to one o' them grand houses on Portman Square. The family jus' now set off fer the country and left a full larder behind. Polly dinna rightly know what to do with all that extra food, so I jus' be helpin' her out a wee bit, ye ken. Put it to good use, like. Never be missed. I'll jus' be about puttin' together a nice stew, shall I?"

"Thank you, MacDougal," Aunt Hetty replied in a wistful tone. "That would be lovely."

MacDougal nodded, turned, and left the room, closing the door quietly behind him.

"Come, come, Aunt Hetty," Catherine said impatiently as her aunt's eyes seemed to gaze into some private distance—no doubt filled with visions of steaming, rich mutton stew. "The envelope, Aunt! The envelope."

"Oh," Aunt Hetty replied, her concentration apparently having returned to the here and now. "Yes, yes. Of course. The envelope." She tapped it gently against her cheek and smiled. "Now what do you think it can be?"

"Aunt Hetty!"

The older woman laughed. "I am only teasing you,

child. I have no notion what it can be, so let us find out."

She carefully opened the seal, unfolded the envelope, and pulled out a large engraved card. "Oh!" she said. "Oh, my. How very nice of her."

"Who is it from, Aunt?" Susannah asked. Apparently her hopes that the carriage might miraculously return had been abandoned, and she came to stand at Catherine's side.

"The Duchess of Carlisle."

Catherine's gasp echoed that of Susannah. Surely she had not heard correctly. "The Duchess of Carlisle?" she asked.

Her aunt smiled and nodded.

"A duchess? Writing to *you*, Aunt Hetty?" Catherine's voice rose in disbelief. "You are not acquainted with her, surely."

"Oh, but I am," her aunt replied, as though it were the most common thing in the world. "We were at school together."

"You know a *real* duchess?" Susannah asked, her blue eyes wide with wonder.

"But you never mentioned it before, Aunt Hetty," Catherine said in an accusatory tone. "Why is it you never mentioned it before?"

"Well, I have not seen her for years. We were together at Miss Darlington's Academy for Young Ladies—more years ago than I care to say."

"You went to school with a *real* duchess?" Susannah asked.

"She was not a duchess at the time, my dear," Aunt Hetty replied. "She was plain Isabelle Montrose. Well, not plain, in any sense, of course. She was a beautiful creature. And she was actually the Honorable Miss Montrose. But then she had the good fortune to attract the attention of the Duke of Carlisle. I saw her only once after that. Just after her wedding. My, but she was a pretty little thing."

"And she writes you now," Catherine said, still incredulous, "out of the blue, after all these years?"

"As it happens," Aunt Hetty said, "I almost literally bumped into her just yesterday, while walking in Green Park with Miss Rathburn. It seems Her Grace is in Town for a few days to see her modiste, and just happened to take the air at the same time as we did." Aunt Hetty chuckled softly and tugged at her cap. "She is as pretty as ever. We had a nice long stroll together and reminisced over old times and old friends. It really was lovely to see her again."

Catherine forced her lips together, for her mouth had dropped open during this extraordinary recital. "You never told us, Aunt!" she exclaimed. "You might have mentioned you had bumped into a duchess, for goodness sake."

"It must have slipped my mind, dear." Aunt Hetty's eyes strayed to the card in her hand, and Catherine knew that no such thing had happened. She had deliberately not mentioned it. But why?

"Well, what does she write, Aunt?" Catherine asked. "What does she say?"

Aunt Hetty heaved a contented sigh and leaned back in her chair. She looked up at her two nieces, her gray eyes twinkling with merriment, before returning her gaze to the vellum card. "It seems I have been invited, along with my two nieces," she said with a nod toward the sisters, "to join in the duchess's annual summer house party at Chissingworth."

A moment of absolute silence followed as both girls stared at her.

"Oh, my *goodness*!" Susannah sank into a chair and gawked at her aunt with eyes like blue saucers. "Oh, my *goodness*."

Catherine studied her aunt for a moment to determine if she might be teasing. But surely she would not tease about such a thing. Surely she would not. Catherine's heart began to pound against her chest, and she sent her aunt an imploring look. When Aunt Hetty nodded and smiled, such a thrill coursed through Catherine's veins that she actually shivered. Clutching her upper arms, she began to bounce slightly on the balls of her feet. "Oh, Aunt Hetty!" she said, barely able to maintain her composure.

Susannah suddenly leaped from her chair with a whoop and tossed her spectacles in the air. Catherine watched as they clattered to the floor—thankfully, unbroken—when she was unexpectedly grabbed by the waist. Susannah twirled her sister around and around in a dance of pure exhilaration. Catherine laughed at her sister's uninhibited, almost childlike joy. Her own spirits were no less ebullient just then, and she allowed herself to become caught up in her sister's excitement.

"Is it not *wonderful*?" Susannah exclaimed as they danced about the room, bumping now and then into a piece of furniture that she could not clearly see until it was too late. "A house party, Cath! A real house party!" A chair overturned with a crash as they collided with it. "Oh, but it will be so much fun!" She spun them around faster and faster. "Fun, fun, *fun*!"

Twirling and laughing until they were dizzy—and slightly bruised—the sisters finally came to a stop in order to catch their breath. Their aunt laughed at their giddiness and clapped her hands. Susannah reached down to give her a hug.

Aunt Hetty looked up at Catherine and raised her brows. "Well, my dear," she said, "Sukey appears to enjoy the notion of a month in the country. What do *you* have to say to the matter?"

Catherine clasped her hands to her chest, still feeling a bit winded. "This is it," she said in a breathless whisper. "This is it. This is it." Her voice rose almost to a squeal. "This is *it*!"

Aunt Hetty raised her brows and nodded in agreement.

"This is what, Cath?" Susannah asked.

Catherine rolled her eyes to the heavens. "The opportunity we have been waiting for, Sukey!"

She grasped the sides of her dress, held them out wide, and began to slowly twirl around the room again all by herself. It was incredible. Truly incredible. Who would have guessed that such good fortune would come their way so easily? Actually presented to them on a silver platter? Unable to contain her excitement, she threw back her head and laughed as she glided about the tiny room, imagining it was the grand ballroom at Chissingworth.

"What opportunity?" Susannah asked.

Catherine stopped in her tracks to glare at her beautiful, thick-headed sister. "To find rich husbands, of course!"

Gravel crunched beneath his heavy boots as the Duke of Carlisle paced back and forth on the garden path. He came to a stop in front of a stone bench and glared down at the woman who sat there.

"Dammit, Mother, this is most inconvenient."

"Oh, do stop fussing, Stephen," the duchess said as she adjusted the angle of her parasol. "It cannot have escaped your notice that we have had a house party here at Chissingworth every August these past twenty years and more."

The duke dug his hands deeper into the pockets of his dirt-smeared smock and made his best effort at appearing to loom over his mother. "I had hoped," he said in his most imperious, ducal voice, "that you would make an exception this year."

The duchess leaned farther back and squinted up at her son, her mouth slightly agape with astonishment. He should have known better than to use that tone with his mother. It had never worked before, probably because she had as much as taught it to him.

"What on earth gave you that idea?" she asked.

"You must know that I cannot abandon my project—"

"Oh! You and your project!" She gave a wave of her hand as if swatting away some annoying insect. "What does that signify?"

"It means I cannot leave Chissingworth. I must supervise the work if it is to be done exactly to my specifications."

"Then stay."

"I would prefer not to," the duke said. "You know I cannot abide these things."

He shuddered as he thought of the wretched hordes descending upon his beloved Chissingworth, posing and preening and prattling, affecting boredom and fashionable ennui while running his poor staff ragged. Worst of all, though, the thing he dreaded more than anything, was playing the role of His Grace before a pack of fawning toadies and sycophants. He would as soon be thrown into a pit of starving rodents.

"You *will* not stay. But you *cannot* go." She rolled her eyes heavenward and clicked her tongue. "What would you have me do?" The duchess glared up at her son with eyes almost the same shade of green as his own. "The invitations have been sent, Stephen. I will not cancel the party because of your infernal glass conservatory. You must do as you wish, my dear, but the party goes on."

Stephen ripped off his wide-brimmed straw hat and slammed it against his thigh with a muttered curse.

The duchess wrinkled her nose at the cloud of dirt that rose from his breeches. "I trust," she said in a reproachful tone, "that you will behave yourself when my guests arrive. And at least *try* to look presentable." She glared down the length of her nose as she surveyed him from head to foot.

For a brief moment he felt like a schoolboy undergoing inspection, and could not help but look down at himself. Sturdy laborers' boots that laced up almost to the knee, dirt-covered chamois breeches, a coarse green smock over a comfortable lawn shirt and Belcher tie. It all seemed presentable enough—the perfect work clothes for a serious gardener. What did a little dirt signify?

"I will do no such thing," he said at last. "If your friends choose to invade my home, to be fed and housed at my expense, then they can bloody well take me as I am. Dirt and all."

His mother's face broke into a dazzling smile. "Splendid!" she said. "Then you will join us after all. I am so pleased, my dear. It has been too long since you have been about in Society. And I have invited a few new faces this year."

"Then I trust, madam, that you will enjoy gazing upon them, for I shall not see them."

"Oh, Stephen!"

"I cannot leave with the new conservatory under construction. But that does not mean that I have any intention of participating in your little gathering. Make no mistake, I shall remain least in sight."

"But, Stephen, I had hoped—"

"And I will not countenance any intrusion upon my privacy," he said, falling once again into his most authoritative ducal voice. "Let me make myself clear upon that point, Mother. As far as your guests are concerned, His Grace is not in residence. And as for you," he added, smiling at the sharp note of challenge in her eye, "well, you need not fear that your eccentric son will be on hand to embarrass you. You see, my dear, it is best for everyone."

"Oh, but, Stephen—"

"I will have your agreement on this matter, Mother."

"But—"

"The duke is not in residence."

The duchess heaved a dramatic sigh. Her shoulders sagged dejectedly and her parasol drooped to the side. Stephen's mouth twitched at the corners as he tried to suppress a grin. He watched as his mother raised a fluttery hand to her breast and cast her eyes to the ground, dark lashes silhouetted against her cheeks. It was no wonder she had been able to talk his late father into doing anything she wanted. The woman was a shameless manipulator. But Stephen was immune to his mother's wiles and would not be coerced in this matter.

He only hoped she would not resort to tears.

"All right, my dear," she said in a thin voice. "If that is what you wish."

Stephen kicked at the gravel with the toe of his boot, annoyed with his mother's tactics. He did not believe her resigned acquiescence for one moment. Nor did he completely trust her. He sincerely hoped she did not have some scheme up her sleeve. "What I wish is that I could leave Chissingworth," he said. "But since that is not possible, this plan will have to do."

How he was to stay out of the way of fifty houseguests he was not quite sure. But somehow, he would contrive to do so. Stephen had avoided polite Society most of his adult life, and so there would likely be many guests who would not recognize him for the duke if they passed him on the street. But for those guests who knew him . . . well, it would only take one sighting to set off the whole lot of them.

And he had no wish to be subject to the fawning and fussing that inevitably followed a presentation to His Grace. He would not be left alone for a single moment if he made an appearance at his mother's party. He would be smothered with attention, pushed and pulled in every direction until he was ready to run screaming from the house. He would be sought out for his opinion on such far-flung subjects as the latest

fashions or the war on the Peninsula; for his endorse-
ment of some new bill before the Lords; for thinly
veiled pleas for funding of Lord So-and-So's pet project; for help in securing some shirttail relation a position. And, most egregious of all, he would be sought
after by every hopeful mother with an unmarried
daughter in tow.

For, besides the Duke of Devonshire—who was
deaf as a post and showed no interest in women—
Stephen was the only bachelor duke in the kingdom.

No, he would stay away once again from his
mother's annual summer gathering. Every year they
had the same argument. And every year, until now,
he had left Chissingworth for one of his other estates.
Just because he could not leave this time made no difference. No amount of his mother's wheedling would
compel him to participate. Not at this house party or
the one next year or the year after that. No, ma'am.

He bowed slightly to his mother, ran his fingers
through his tousled brown hair, and plopped the
straw hat back upon his head. "Until further notice,
then," he said, "the Duke of Carlisle is not in residence."

He turned on his heel and headed down the gravel
path. A niggling twinge of doubt pursued him
through the rose garden, buzzing in his ear like a
pesky gnat. He began to wonder if he was making a
huge mistake.

Perhaps he ought to abandon his precious glass
conservatory after all and run for his life.

Chapter 2

Susannah and Aunt Hetty easily fell in with Catherine's plan to use the Chissingworth party to their advantage. However, each of them became so caught up in the excitement of their prospects that it was left to Catherine to maintain a cool head in facing the endless problems involved in a month's stay at an elegant country estate. What to wear and how to get there were the most pressing issues at hand.

"We must have clothes!" she announced soon after they had made the decision to attend the party. "The right clothes. It will not be worth going at all if we are to appear as shabby genteel outsiders. The sort of gentlemen most likely to be at Chissingworth would be scornful of our poverty."

"We cannot help it if we are poor," Susannah replied.

"No, of course we cannot," Catherine said. "But there is no reason to be announcing it to all the world. We must disguise our situation as best we can. We must give every appearance of at least comfortable circumstances. Else we will surely be seen as encroaching fortune hunters."

Aunt Hetty arched a brow and Catherine felt a

blush color her cheeks. "There is no need to give me that look, Aunt," she said. "I know what you are thinking. I know. We *are* encroaching fortune hunters. But only because Papa left us in such a mess. It is not as if we were cits, or anything like that," she said, wrinkling her nose in distaste. "It is not *our* fault he got caught up in yet another of those wretched investment bubbles. We cannot be blamed for his irresponsibility. Or his cowardice," she added in an undertone.

She plopped into a chair in a most unladylike manner, threw her head against the rail back, and heaved a sigh. "I am so tired of living like church mice, scraping just to get by. But the only way out I can foresee is for one of us to secure an advantageous marriage. You must see how important this party is, Aunt Hetty."

"Of course I do, my dear. Of course I do."

"And Susannah is so lovely she is bound to attract admirers at such a party." She turned toward her sister, whose bright blue eyes looked wide with wonder and artless innocence. Catherine knew, however, that the look was born of nearsightedness, not wonder. But it gave Susannah an air of ingenuousness, an almost angelic quality that only served to enhance her beauty. She was sure to draw the attention of every gentleman at Chissingworth. But he must be the right sort of gentleman.

"You must always remember, Sukey, what we are about," Catherine said. "Your beauty will lure gentlemen to your side, but you must be sure to avoid the wrong sorts."

"What sorts?" Susannah asked.

Catherine sighed. All God's energy had been spent providing her elder sister with such stunning looks that He had neglected to provide her with any intellect to speak of. She would have to keep a very close watch on Susannah if this plan was to work at all.

"Penniless younger sons, clerics, half-pay officers, that sort," she replied. "Try to remember, Sukey, that it is not just any husband, but a rich husband that we seek. I am counting on you, my dear. You may be our only hope."

Susannah sat up straight and raised her chin a notch. "I will do my best," she said in as determined a tone as her breathy, girlish soprano allowed. "I am tired of being poor, too, you know. But I *will* do my best. If only I can marry well, then I can bring you and Aunt Hetty to live with me. Then it should be an easy enough thing to find a husband for you, too, Cath. And maybe even for you, too, Aunt Hetty!"

All three ladies laughed at such an absurd notion. But soon enough, Susannah's brow beetled up in a look of confusion. "But how will I know who is rich and who is not?" she asked.

"You must leave that to me and Aunt Hetty," Catherine said, not for a moment trusting that Susannah could be left to decide such matters for herself. "Remain aloof to any gentleman who gives you his attention until one of us can verify his circumstances. We will tell you who to avoid and who to encourage."

Susannah reached over and grabbed her sister's hand and squeezed it affectionately. "Dear Cath. I wish I were as clever as you. I will not do anything without consulting you first. I promise."

Catherine smiled, as she always did when those big blue eyes were turned on her with such sincerity. Susannah might not be the brightest star in the firmament, but she meant well. She was as sweet-natured as she was beautiful, and Catherine loved her dearly. "I am sure every unmarried gentleman at Chissingworth will fall in love with you, Sukey," she said. "How could they not?"

"Perhaps even the duke himself will fall in love with one of you," Aunt Hetty added with a twinkle in her eye as she looked up from her darning.

Catherine laughed. "Heavens, Aunt! We cannot expect such a sacrifice from poor Sukey. We want her to marry a rich man, but not if he's touched in the head."

"Touched in the head?" Aunt Hetty asked, her eyes widening in astonishment. "Whatever do you mean?"

"Don't be coy, Aunt Hetty. You know as well as the next person that the Duke of Carlisle is a notorious eccentric at best. He keeps so much to himself that he hasn't been seen for years—despite the fact that his mother is an important figure in Society and seen everywhere. There are even rumors that the poor man is unbalanced and kept locked away by his family."

"Oh, fustian!" Aunt Hetty said with a dismissive wave of her hand. "That is the most ridiculous thing I have ever heard. The Duke of Carlisle, unbalanced? Unlikely, my dear. Not if his mother had any say in the matter."

"Well, in any case," Catherine continued, "we must not expect him to be at his mother's house party. But it does not signify. There will surely be plenty of other eligible gentlemen in attendance. But just now," she said as she rose from her chair, "we must concern ourselves with our wardrobes. Come, Sukey, let us rummage through Mama's trunks to see what we can salvage."

In short order, the two sisters were on their knees in the tiny, dingy attic, sorting through stacks of old-fashioned gowns that had belonged to their late mother and even some that dated back to their grandmother. Many were from the last century with long, tight-fitting bodices and would be difficult to alter. Fortunately, however, Susannah's one great talent in life, besides looking beautiful, was as an expert seamstress. With the proper materials at hand and her spectacles perched on her nose, she could fashion a gown that exactly copied those in the ladies' magazines, a gown that looked as if it had come from the finest modiste.

And so, while Catherine sought out bits of ribbon, lace, or other trim that could be salvaged from the most worn pieces, Susannah examined the better pieces and determined which bodices could be raised, which skirts layered or lowered.

Catherine looked up from her work at the sound of a sudden racket coming from below. Heavy footsteps could be heard making their way up the narrow staircase, accompanied by regular grunts and groans and the occasional crash, as though something substantial had struck the wall. Catherine glanced at Susannah, thinking she might know what on earth was going on, but her sister just pushed aside a stray blond curl and shook her head. Catherine turned back toward the stairs in time to see MacDougal and an unknown young man navigating a huge trunk around the final landing and into the small attic room where she and Susannah sat. The men dropped the trunk with a loud crash.

"Och! Here ye be, ladies," MacDougal said in a winded voice as he wiped the back of his hand across his brow. "Thought ye might be able to make some use o' these few things."

"What have you there, MacDougal?" Catherine asked.

"This here, ye ken, is me cousin Dermott MacDougal," he said. The young man nodded self-consciously and stepped back into the shadows. His eyes darted every few seconds toward Susannah. "He works over to Lord Fairchild's, he does. Footman now, but butler one day, ye mark my words."

The young man hung his head and blushed.

"Anyhow," MacDougal continued, "his lordship had three daughters, ye ken. All married now, verra well placed, they be. But they left behind these few bits of gowns and such. Dermott here says they be packed away up there in that attic doin' nobody any good, just waitin' to be hauled off fer some charitable cause or other. Could be they're a bit out of fashion—I dinna know about them things meself, ye ken. But we figured as how they're wasted in his lordship's attic, and ye young ladies might be able to make some use of 'em."

Susannah had risen while MacDougal spoke and walked to the trunk. Young Dermott MacDougal, his eyes wide with admiration, reached down to open it for her.

"Oh, my *goodness!*" she exclaimed when the lid had been thrown back.

Catherine rose, brushed off her skirts, and joined Susannah. She stifled a gasp at the sight before her. A beautiful green sarsnet gown lay folded neatly in tissue at the top of the trunk. Susannah carefully pulled it out, oohing and ahhing as she gently held up the elegant creation. Catherine's eyes strayed back to the trunk, where a dress of fine white India muslin sprigged with tiny embroidered white flowers sat for her inspection. More dresses followed. Silks and lutestrings, merinos and crepes, satins and muslins. It was a magnificent collection that quite took her breath away.

"Oh, but, MacDougal," she said at last, "we cannot take these things. They belong to the Fairchilds."

"No more daughters at home, miss," he replied. "And Lady Fairchild's too stout by half to fit into any o' them dresses. Too fine fer the housemaids. The Fairchilds have no use fer 'em, mark me words. Dinna they mean to have 'em carted off anyway? Trust me. They'll never be missed."

Catherine eyed him skeptically. She didn't quite trust him, but neither could she afford to reject such an unexpected bounty. "You are sure, MacDougal? You are sure it is all right?"

"Oh, Cath, just *look* at them!" Susannah exclaimed. "They may need a bit of alteration here and there, some updated trim, some new lace. But, oh, Cath, they're beautiful. Just beautiful. Can we keep them? Can we?"

"Of course ye can," MacDougal answered. "Nothing but the best fer you lassies. And besides," he said with a grin, "they'll never be missed."

Without another word, MacDougal and his young cousin turned and headed for the landing and then down the stairs.

They'll never be missed.

I certainly hope not, Catherine thought as she joined her sister in sorting the rest of the dresses from the trunk.

"Let us drink to my last day of peace." Stephen said as he raised his rummer of port. "The hordes descend on the morrow, and I shall not see the inside of my own dining room for the next month."

"To peace, then," said his friend Miles, the Earl of Strickland, raising his own glass to clank against Stephen's.

Stephen took a long swallow, dropped his glass heavily upon the polished mahogany table, and sank back comfortably in his chair. It was good to spend time with Miles again. The earl was Stephen's closest friend—almost his only friend, in fact. He had been invited by the duchess to join in the house party and had arrived a few days early.

"I don't suppose it is worth trying to change your mind?" the earl asked.

"About what?" Stephen replied. "Taking part in Mother's wretched gathering? Don't waste your breath, Miles. You should know me better than that."

Miles shrugged and chuckled softly. "It was worth a try," he said. "I know you loathe this sort of thing, but I had hoped . . . well, I had hoped." He took another swallow of port. "Now that I have seen the conservatory construction, I can understand why you could not bring yourself to leave. It is going to be magnificent."

"I think so," Stephen said. "I am in great need of a larger space for my experiments as well as the more tropical specimens."

"It will be a handsome building."

Stephen laughed. "Repton would not agree. He would have had me make it an extension of the house, an uninterrupted organic flow from interior to conservatory to garden. Can you imagine me slapping such a thoroughly modern structure onto Chissingworth? Ha! My ancestors would come back to haunt me for such an affront. Besides, it is not meant to be a picturesque decoration. It has a function, for God's sake. Repton would have me plop a handful of thatch on its roof and call it an ornamental dairy." He shuddered at the very notion.

Miles laughed. "I must say that I rather admire what he has done at Woburn and Stoneleigh. But, in this case, I have to agree with you. It would be almost criminal to force a sort of rustic informality on Chissingworth. It is a grand estate and ought to remain so."

"Thank you, my friend." Stephen reached for the port, refilled each of their rummers, and returned the decanter to the pierced silver wine coaster. "I am pleased you have come, Miles," he said. "I hadn't known that Mother invited you. I am glad she did. It has been too long since you have paid us a visit."

"To tell the truth, I almost did not come," Miles said. "I do so hate to leave the girls for very long. But two things decided it for me. When I heard you were not planning to bolt this year—your mother enclosed a note with the invitation—I decided I had kept myself cooped up at Epping far too long. I wanted to be with friends again. Of course, I did not really expect you would participate in the party. I do know you better than that, you see. But I thought I might be able to sneak away from the other guests now and then and beard the absent lion in his den, so to speak. That is, if you can be torn away from your conservatory long enough to share an occasional brandy. You do recall that I know of the secret door to your office."

"And you are welcome to use it, my friend," Stephen said. "So long as it remains a secret to the other guests. It is the only safe haven I can imagine during the next month."

"Indeed," Miles said. "For who would expect the Duke of Carlisle, owner and resident of one of the largest estates in the land, to work in a small, cluttered office tucked away behind the old conservatory? Any duke worth his salt would have a spacious library office—Gibbons paneling, walls of glass-enclosed bookshelves, an enormous, but very tidy, carved oak desk, an old master or two staring down from the walls. You know the sort of thing."

"Yes." Stephen laughed. "Rather like your own office at Epping, I should think."

"Exactly," Miles replied with a grin. "It does wonders for one's consequence to be surrounded by such grandeur. But there you are in your cubbyhole of an office—"

"It's not that small!"

"—with a desk whose surface you probably have not seen in twenty years, surrounded by mountains of books and pamphlets and drawings. Yes, Stephen, I should think you will be very safe in your office. No one would dream of finding His Grace in such a place."

"And I do not have to act as His Grace when I am working there," Stephen said.

"Which is no doubt why you spend so much time there."

Stephen grinned and shrugged. "No doubt," he said. "But you mentioned two reasons for coming, Miles. What was the other?"

Miles took a long swallow of port and replaced the

glass carefully upon the table. He kept his hand about its stem, however, and did not look up. He cleared his throat nervously. "I . . . I have decided to marry again."

"Miles! But that is wonderful," Stephen said as he clapped his friend soundly upon the back. "I am so pleased for you. I had not thought . . . I did not expect you would ever . . . Oh, for God's sake, man! Who is she?"

Miles looked up with an uncharacteristically sheepish grin. "I . . . um . . . don't know yet," he said, running his fingers absently up and down the stem of the glass. "That is why I have come, you see. I thought I might begin my search here at Chissingworth. Your mother always used to invite several unattached young ladies to her summer gatherings, as I recall."

"Yes," Stephen said, "in hopes of luring me to stay and join in." He studied his friend closely, surprised to think that he might want to marry again. There was no possibility that Miles was joking. He was a fine man and a good friend, but not one given to lighthearted jesting. Of course, he had little to be lighthearted about. Stephen took another sip of port. "I must say, Miles," he continued, "you have taken me quite by surprise. I had no idea you wished to remarry."

Miles leaned back in his chair, ran a hand through his short-cropped dark hair, and sighed. A shadow of sadness gathered in his eyes for the briefest moment before he shrugged it away. "I had not thought I ever would," he said. "Amelia was the one true love of my life, as you well know. I would never try to replace her. But the girls . . . ah, Stephen, they are so sweet and so precious to me. But so very young. They need a mother."

"So you are tossing yourself back into the fray for the sake of your daughters?"

Miles chuckled softly. "I hadn't actually considered

it in such frightening terms. But I suppose you are right. I have not been at all looking forward to reentering the Marriage Mart. The whole notion only brings on waves of melancholy as I recall that Season when I first met Amelia."

He paused, and his eyes stared off into some private distance. Stephen did not disrupt his friend's reverie. He knew that grief still held hold of Miles's heart, and Stephen had never known quite what to say to ease the pain. Never having loved deeply, he could not imagine the effect of such a loss. He had tried to be a good friend to Miles during those awful months after Amelia's death two years ago, but he had never felt adequate to the task. What can one ever do or say to a friend whose heart and life have been shattered?

He had once envied his friend's love match. He had wondered what it would be like to love like that. But he no longer pondered such things. Stephen had never allowed himself to love a woman, and never would, for he would never be able to believe that she really loved him and not only his title and fortune. Almost every time he had ever been introduced to a young woman, he caught a glimmer of avaricious interest in her eyes before it could be masked with civility. It was always the same. And always would be. He had once envied Miles, but would rather never love at all than to love without being able to trust that it was truly returned. A ridiculous conviction, no doubt. But there it was.

Miles shook his head and then took another swallow of port. "Anyway," he continued at last, sounding more in control, "now that I have made the decision to marry again, I was hoping to ease into things gently, so to speak. Perhaps make the acquaintance of a few young ladies here at Chissingworth, without actually announcing that I am in the market for a wife. Who knows? I may meet just the girl right here, and never have to suffer through a Season in Town."

"If that is what you want, old chap, then I wish you good luck," Stephen said, raising his rummer in salute.

"It is what I want, Stephen. Truly. I need a mother for my daughters."

"And what of yourself?" Stephen asked. "You will be getting more than a nursemaid for the girls. She will be your wife. Your countess."

"Yes, of course, and I will do everything I can to make her comfortable and content. And I . . . well, I will not miss the loneliness, I suppose. But do not think, Stephen, that I look for another love match. That will not happen."

"I know that, Miles. I do. Just be sure to look to your own needs as well as those of your girls. And I do wish you luck, my friend. I am not privy to Mother's guest list, but she did mention something about a few new faces this year. Perhaps you will find one of them suitable."

"I hope so," Miles said. "Oh, but please do not tell the duchess of my plans. She is a dear lady, your mother, but . . ."

Stephen laughed. "I know. She can be an unstoppable force once she gets a bee in her bonnet. It would never do to give her any matchmaking ideas. Not to worry. She shall hear nothing from me."

"Thank you. I should like to go about this rather slowly, at my own pace." Miles heaved another sigh. "God, Stephen, it's been so long since I've even looked at another woman—I hope I haven't forgot how to do this."

Stephen laughed. "I am certain it will all come back to you, old man."

Chapter 3

The late afternoon sun still hung high in the summer sky as the carriage approached the gatehouse of Chissingworth. Catherine sent up yet another silent prayer of thanks that the great estate was located in the uplands of Kent and so only a day's drive from Chelsea. She shuddered to think what measures would have been required if they had had to stay overnight on the road.

The massive Tudor gatehouse—Catherine knew it to be Tudor for she had looked up Chissingworth in the *Beauties of England and Wales* at the Chelsea Lending Library—included four battlemented corner turrets and a pointed arch entry surmounted by a carved heraldic shield. The shield included two facing lions, and Catherine recognized it from the seal on the duchess's invitation. The Carlisle coat of arms, apparently.

After a word from MacDougal, the gatekeeper waved them through. As the carriage lurched forward Catherine's shoulder bumped against that of young Molly Finucane, the young niece of MacDougal, who was to maid them during their stay at Chissingworth. Molly smiled shyly and then returned her attention to the passing scenery. Susannah, sitting on the opposite seat with Aunt Hetty, also stared wide-eyed out the carriage window, her spectacles firmly in place so that she would miss nothing as they entered the grounds of the estate. Catherine turned her own gaze toward the sprawling woodlands as her fingers trailed lightly along the rich velvet of the softly up-holstered squabs.

'Tis indeed a wonder, she thought, that she and Su-sannah and Aunt Hetty should be entering one of the grandest estates in the kingdom as invited guests, traveling in an elegantly appointed, well-sprung coach, wearing fashionable gowns, and accompanied by their personal maid. Thanks to the efforts of Mac-Dougal, no one would guess that only this morning they had been simply three impoverished ladies of no consequence living in Chelsea.

Catherine and Aunt Hetty had scraped together just enough money to take them by mail coach to Maidstone, and from there to hire a post chaise to carry them the rest of the way to Chissingworth. Aunt Hetty had argued that they could not afford a post chaise, and that the duchess would be happy to send a carriage for them to the nearby village of Hitchcock. But Catherine had been adamant that they arrive in a private carriage. She would have been mortified to have it known that the Forsythe sisters had arrived with the mail. And so she had compromised by agree-ing to take the mail coach as far as Maidstone.

In the end, however, they had been saved from spending what little money they had. The day before, MacDougal had pulled up in front of the tiny house on Flood Street, bold as brass, driving a splendid coach and four.

"Me cousin, Robby MacDougal," he had announced, "keeps the stables and carriage house over to Lord Pe-tersham's in Cavendish Square. His lordship's off to Italy wi' Lady Petersham—her health bein' delicate and all that, he wanted to get her away from the damp, ye ken." MacDougal's eyes crinkled up in the corners as he smiled at Catherine. "Aye, and so, there be all them fine carriages just sittin' there gatherin' dust, and horses just pinin' for a good exercise. We be doin' his lordship a favor by taking 'em out, keepin' 'em fit and healthy. And wi' him in Italy, why, they'll never be missed."

Catherine had strongly objected. There were, after all, limits to how far she was willing to go in her pretense of a comfortable fortune. "This isn't like a stack of discarded dresses that could be altered, MacDougal," she had argued. "I am sure Lord Petersham has no intention of discarding his carriages. And we certainly cannot alter them. You had no right taking them. You must return them at once."

"Weel, noo," he had said, rubbing his chin and narrowing his eyes, "the fact is Robby's in charge while his lordship be away. The horses and the carriages be in his care, ye ken. If Robby's willin' to let us borrow 'em, who are we to argue? He says he'll take full responsibility, so there ye have it."

Catherine had still not been completely convinced. It was surely tempting and could be the answer to their dilemma, but the last thing she wanted was to be caught out in a charade.

"Lord Petersham's crest is there on the carriage door for all the world to see," she said. "How do we explain arriving at Chissingworth in his lordship's carriage? We cannot say we just borrowed it. What if one of his acquaintances is among the guests?"

MacDougal smiled again and his dark eyes glittered with triumph. "Dinna worrit yerself, Miss Catherine. Look here."

He reached inside the carriage and retrieved a plain black wooden panel. While Catherine watched, bewildered, he anchored the panel between two grooves at opposite sides of the window's edge. With only a slight push from the top, the panel slid down between the grooves, stopping with a loud clack as it landed against a small ridge along the bottom edge of the door. Catherine had gaped in astonishment to see a plain black coach where once had stood the crested Petersham carriage.

"Good heavens!" Catherine had exclaimed. "What—"

"Apparently Lord Petersham likes to be anonymous now and again," MacDougal said.

"But I do not understand—"

"Dinna ask too many questions, Miss Catherine. 'Tis no' a subject fit fer a young lass such as yerself."

"Oh." Catherine said no more, though she would have liked to pursue such an interesting topic. In the end she had accepted the use of the carriage with gratitude. And with MacDougal to act as coachman. He had even gone so far as to borrow from his cousin a striped waistcoat and black top hat, so that he looked every inch the professional whip. As the carriage hugged the winding road that snaked through the woodlands of Chissingworth, Catherine had to admire MacDougal's prowess with the ribbons, and wondered once again where he had come by his many talents.

Later that same day, after "borrowing" Lord Petersham's carriage, MacDougal had presented them with Molly.

"She be m' sister Lizzy's girl," he had said. "The wee lass be only fifteen, but she's been workin' as a tweenie at Sir Horace Drummond's place, where Lizzy's the head house parlor maid. Molly here wants to be a lady's maid one day, don't ye, girl?"

"Oh, yes!" she replied. "'Tis what I want more than anything in the whole world."

"And so," MacDougal continued, "she be willin' to work fer ye ladies, so long as ye dinna mind her practicin' on ye. I reckon it'd be good trainin', doin' fer all three of ye ladies while ye be away. I told Molly ye

prob'ly wouldna mind her bein' inexperienced and
all. And I told her she shouldna be expectin' any pay,
since she'd only be practicin' and all. Ain't that right,
Molly girl?"

"Oh no, 'twouldn't be right to pay me whilst I be
just learnin'," she said.

Catherine had been overwhelmed that MacDougal
had made such an arrangement for them. More than
anyone, he knew the extent of their straitened circumstances, and he had gone out of his way to make this
trip to Chissingworth successful. But Catherine had
not felt entirely comfortable with the arrangement
with Molly, thinking that they would be taking advantage of the girl, when she could be making at least
a small salary somewhere else. She had opened her
mouth to protest when MacDougal had stopped her
short.

"Dinna fret about not payin' the girl," he said, as
though reading her very thoughts. "We'll find her a
decent meal and a place to sleep in the servants' quarters and she'll be fine. And I'll be there to look out fer
her. Promised Lizzy I would. Besides, she couldna expect to ever get maidin' experience anywheres else.
No' at her age. She'd have to work her way up, like,
over the years. Nae, this is the best thing coulda happened, ain't it, Molly m'girl?"

"Oh, yes," Molly replied in an anxious voice. "I'd
be that grateful if you'd let me maid for you. And I
promise to work real hard and learn ever so quick."

Aunt Hetty had gratefully accepted Molly's offer
on behalf of all three of them before Catherine could
protest further. And so it had been settled. Young
Molly had not exaggerated her willingness to work
hard. She had been a great help to them as they had
packed their trunks for the trip. With the castoffs from
the Fairchild daughters, the wardrobes of all three
ladies had grown tremendously.

And so, here they were, three impoverished ladies

from Flood Street, in a fine carriage with fine clothes and a personal maid.

And one other thing. Catherine glanced at the small wooden case on Molly's lap. One other small detail for which they must once again thank MacDougal.

This time he had gone straight to Aunt Hetty rather than risk any argument from Catherine. Her ever-so-obliging aunt had shown no scruples about accepting the small case of jewelry.

Like the carriage, the jewelry had been temporarily "borrowed" from an absent household where one of MacDougal's ubiquitous relatives was employed. The mistress of the house had, of course, taken her best pieces along with her. But the few baubles left behind were good quality and not at all showy, and, according to MacDougal, would never be missed.

By the time the thick woodlands had given way to broad expanses of green parkland, Catherine was full of conviction that not a single guest would question their circumstances. Everything had been perfectly arranged, thanks in large part to the wily MacDougal. It was going to work. There was no question in her mind. It was going to work.

When a slight rise dipped away to reveal their first glimpse of the great house, Susannah gasped audibly.

"My goodness!" she exclaimed in a breathless voice. "Oh, my goodness! Is it not wonderful? And so large! Have you ever seen anything so grand in your entire life, Aunt Hetty? Oh, Cath, is it not beautiful?"

"It certainly is," Catherine replied, for once in perfect agreement with her sister's hyperbole. In the distance, the house sat in solitary splendor amidst sweeping green lawns dotted here and there with clusters of ash trees. Red and fallow deer grazed peacefully in small groups, some lying in the shade of the trees, their heads jerking to attention at the sound of the passing carriage. A narrow tributary of the River Beult, just ahead, was spanned by a gracefully

arched stone bridge. Just then, the road curved
sharply to the left and Catherine could see that they
were to cross the bridge.

The impressive north front with its grand Palladian
façade and pedimented entrance disappeared from
view as the carriage approached the older, turreted
west front. MacDougal reined in the horses as elaborate iron gates were swung back from an enormous
arched gateway. The carriage easily cleared the entrance, which opened onto a large courtyard. What
was apparently the main entrance to the house was at
the opposite end, and echoed the appearance of the
outer gate. Two domed turrets stood on either side of
the pointed archway of the central entry. Three stories
of mullioned windows topped with fanciful crenella-
tion flanked the entrance.

As the carriage pulled up before the steps of the
entry, huge oaken doors swung wide, and a coterie of
liveried footmen spilled out. Some went to the horses'
heads, some scurried up to the top of the coach to
begin unloading the baggage, while two others
handed the ladies down. A tall, thin woman in black
appeared and began directing the disposition of the
baggage. Another smaller woman dressed in a fashionable pink muslin gown floated down the steps to
greet them.

"How glad I am to see you, Hetty," she said. "Welcome to Chissingworth." She reached out and em-
braced Aunt Hetty, and Catherine decided this must
be the duchess. She looked much younger than Aunt
Hetty, though they must be of an age since they were
at school together. The duchess, however, had never
faced the sort of financial hardships that had plagued
their aunt. Such trials exact a physical toll as well as
an emotional one. Nonetheless, the duchess was an
extraordinarily beautiful woman, even at her age. Her
rich chestnut hair showed only a very few strands of
silver. Her eyes were a striking shade of green, and

her skin was still clear and smooth with only faint creases around her eyes and mouth.

Catherine glanced over at Susannah, who had removed her spectacles and was looking as wide-eyed and beguiling as ever, and wondered if her sister's beauty would endure with age. There was certainly a better chance of it if she was settled comfortably in an advantageous marriage. Catherine was more determined than ever at that moment to ensure that Susannah stayed beautiful and happy for years to come. She would not leave Chissingworth without contracting a good match for her sister. She would not.

Aunt Hetty presented Catherine and Susannah to the duchess, and each of them curtsied.

"My, but aren't you both pretty?" the duchess said, smiling brightly at each of the sisters. "The gentlemen will be especially pleased to have two such beauties among the guests. What a stroke of luck to run into your aunt so that I might invite you to join us. The other guests will think me so clever for having found you!"

The duchess ushered them into the entry hall, which was at least twice the size of their entire house in Flood Street, and Catherine heard a soft gasp from Susannah.

"It *is* quite daunting, is it not?" The duchess chuckled merrily as she glanced around the hall. "I had the same reaction, Miss Forsythe, the first time I saw it. It is called the Hall of the Caesars, after all the marble busts in the niches along the walls. And the paintings on the ceiling and along the upper walls depict scenes from the life of Julius Caesar. But do not be discouraged, my dears. Not all of Chissingworth is quite so grand. We live quite comfortably, as you shall see." She smiled and patted Susannah's hand.

"Now," she continued, motioning toward the thin woman in black, "Mrs. Beddowes will show you to your rooms. I would be pleased to have you all join me for tea in my sitting room after you've had time to refresh yourselves. I should like to become better acquainted with your beautiful nieces, Hetty, before they become monopolized by the other guests."

Catherine was amazed and delighted to find that she and Susannah and Aunt Hetty each had a private bedchamber. Good heavens, the place must be huge if every guest was so accommodated. Catherine's room was spacious and beautifully decorated, with green silk bed curtains and Chinese painted wallpaper. The friendly reception by the duchess and the lovely bedchamber served to bolster Catherine's confidence. Her plans could not be off to a better start.

And it only got better and better. They spent an hour in the duchess's private sitting room while she and Aunt Hetty recounted tales of their school days. Catherine liked the duchess immensely. She was friendly and open and not at all starchy, as one might expect of a duchess. And it certainly did her no little credit that she frequently mentioned certain gentlemen guests—unmarried gentlemen guests—whose acquaintance she was sure the Forsythe sisters would be pleased to make.

Not all the guests had yet arrived, but by the time Catherine and her family were seated for dinner that evening, they had been introduced to no less than six unmarried gentlemen. Six perfectly eligible, plump-in-the-pocket, titled unmarried gentlemen.

It was going to be a grand month in the country.

Chapter 4

The following morning Catherine slipped away on her own to explore the famous Chissingworth gardens. Before leaving the house, she had given Susannah a stern lecture against allowing any unknown gentleman to become too friendly before they had discovered his circumstances. She had left her in hopefully safe conversation with Aunt Hetty and the duchess. Between her aunt and MacDougal, Catherine had no doubt she would soon be in possession of the facts of the financial situation for each single gentleman in attendance. Her spirits were high as she left the house, confident that the selection of wealthy gentlemen at Chissingworth would afford at least one sister a proper husband.

But just now, as she strolled from the east wing along smooth gravel paths and sheltered shrubbery walks, Catherine found another reason to be grateful for the duchess's invitation. Oh, but it was grand to be back in the country again! To smell clean air, fragrant of summer blossoms and wood smoke. To enjoy clear, blue skies unblemished with coal soot, and sweeping expanses of brilliant green parklands. To have so much space to oneself.

Catherine had not realized how much she missed the country. She had not been out of Chelsea since going there to live with Aunt Hetty after her father's death. Dorland, the small Forsythe estate in Wiltshire, had been lost along with everything else when their father died. All her young life she had longed for a Season in Town, but Sir Benjamin Forsythe's precarious finances had never allowed it. More than two years of scraping to make ends meet in Chelsea, however, had shattered any romantical notions she might have once held regarding the glories of London. Oh, there were glories to be seen in Town, to be sure; but not for the likes of impoverished single ladies in Flood Street.

Perhaps if—when!—she and Susannah contrived to find rich husbands at Chissingworth, she would not mind so much going back to London. In style, this time.

At the moment, she was simply happy to be back in the country. Chissingworth was famous for its gardens and Catherine was anxious to see as much of them as possible. She loved flowers of all kinds, especially wildflowers. At Dorland, one of her greatest pleasures had been painting detailed watercolors of her favorite blossoms. She still kept a portfolio of her paintings of which she was really quite proud.

It had been a long time since she had been able to afford paints and brushes and decent parchment. But she had brought along to Chissingworth a few rolls of foolscap and two or three pencils, one of which was tucked in her pocket at the moment. She harbored secret hopes of finding new and unusual specimens to sketch while in residence at the famous estate.

With this in mind, she wandered through the surprisingly informal arrangement of gardens. In the dressed grounds nearest the house, high, clipped shrubbery hedges of sweetbrier, box, and hawthorn surrounded each garden. Moving through the enclosed hedges was akin to walking through the various rooms of a house, each room different from the last. One was awash in the bright colors of summer, the gravel paths bordered with stocks, pinks, double rocket, sweet williams, and asters. The morning sun fell upon spires of delphinium sparkling with dew. Her artist's eye was drawn to the glitter of moisture on the indigo and royal peaks, and she paused to seat herself on a nearby stone bench. She pulled a pencil and scrap of paper from her pocket and roughly sketched the familiar blossoms.

After a few moments, Catherine moved on to the next garden, which was devoted to roses of all shades. She tilted her head back, closed her eyes, and breathed in the heady fragrance of so many blossoms. She did not, though, stop to draw any of the roses. She instead wandered through a break in the hedge to another garden, this one laid out in a large circle. The plantings graduated in height, from tiny candytuft and sweet mignonette, to lupins, poppies, mallows, and sweet peas. Towering above them all in the center were enormous sunflowers. Catherine was much taken with the harmonious arrangement of such humble varieties as she slowly skirted the circular path, looking for a specimen that she might want to capture on paper.

"Oh! How wonderful!" she exclaimed as she came upon a patch of sweet violets flourishing in the shade of the larger plants. Kneeling down, she carefully caressed the dark purple blossoms of what could only be a pure *viola odorata*. She had never actually seen one before, most common violets being hybrids of other *violaceae*. But she recognized the pure ancestor of the ordinary sweet violet from pictures in one of the illustrated flower books she had once owned. I must sketch this one, she thought. Perhaps if she made a detailed-enough sketch, she would one day be able to paint it in color, from memory. Leaning in closer, she began to carefully examine the soft, fragile petals, holding the blossom ever so gently between her fingers.

And suddenly, she was knocked backward with a thud. *What on earth?*

"Damnation!" muttered the man who had apparently come careening around the garden path directly into her. He grabbed at Catherine's shoulders in an attempt to balance himself.

Instead, he knocked her flat on her back and fell directly on top of her.

Catherine gasped, her face crushed against a dirt-covered smock. "Get off me, you oaf!" she sputtered, pushing against the man's chest.

Muttering something unintelligible, he raised himself slightly and looked down at her. His hat had been knocked away and a curl of dark brown hair fell over his furrowed brow. Green eyes flickered with annoyance and his mouth was a thin line of irritation. But the most noticeable thing about the man at the moment was his weight, which was crushing the breath right out of her. "Get off!" she repeated.

Stephen gazed down into the flashing eyes of a very pretty little termagant. *Bloody hell!* He was in for it now, for she was no doubt one of his mother's guests. He hadn't expected anyone in the gardens this early. He had not been paying much attention to the path, his eyes surveying the center garden as he hurried past. He had not seen the girl as she knelt down at the edge of the gravel walk. And here he was sprawled atop her in a most improper manner.

If it wasn't so awkward, he might be tempted to enjoy it for a moment. She really was very pretty. Dark blond curls were revealed beneath the bonnet that had been knocked askew. Her brows and eyelashes were a much darker color, providing a striking contrast to her fair hair. Her eyes, framed by the long, dark lashes, appeared to be gray.

She really was very pretty.

"Get off me!" she repeated in a choked voice.

Coming to his senses, he realized he must be practically smothering her, so he quickly rolled to the side. "I beg your pardon," he said as he struggled ungracefully to his feet. He extended a hand to help her up. "I am terribly sorry. Are you quite all right?"

She grabbed his hand and allowed him to pull her to a sitting position. She neither looked at him nor answered him, but adjusted her bonnet. "You might have looked where you were going!" she said in a petulant tone. She sat up on her knees and Stephen offered his hand again. She took it, pulled herself upright, then immediately dropped it to shake out her skirts.

"I am terribly sorry," he repeated, brushing himself off and searching the area for his hat. He did not know what else to say. He was reluctant to get into a conversation with the young woman, attractive though she may be. If she recognized him as the duke—which she had thankfully not yet done—there was no telling what sort of fuss she would make. He must get away as quickly as possible before the chit realized who he was and went squealing off to the other guests that she had sighted the elusive duke.

Damn his mother and her parties, anyway. Why couldn't they leave him in peace to putter in his gardens?

"I am so sorry," he said again, trying to keep the annoyance out of his voice as he retrieved his broadbrimmed straw hat from beneath a patch of blue gentian. He slapped it against his thigh a few times and plopped it back upon his head. "It was my fault completely. I trust you are uninjured?"

"I am fine," she said, still straightening her skirts and not looking at him. Stephen's stomach seized up with the notion that she had not yet got a good look at him. There was still a chance she might recognize him. "No thanks to you," she continued in that irritated tone. "And *of course* it was your fault. I was simply minding my own business, admiring the—" She stopped as she looked down at her hand. "Oh, dear."

Stephen moved closer, thinking she might have injured her hand and cursing himself for his own carelessness. "What is it?" he asked. "Have you—" He paused as he saw that she was not injured, but was holding on to a crushed purple blossom.

Good God! It was one of his violets.

His prized, rare, pure-bred violets.

Forgetting for a moment his own culpability, he raged at the girl. "How *dare* you pick my flowers without asking! Do you think these are placed here for anyone to pluck at will? Don't you know—"

"*Your* flowers?" she said, her eyes widening in surprise.

Good Lord. He had given himself away. What an idiot! He was in for it, now.

But his poor violets.

"Oh! You must be the gardener," she said.

The gardener? Looking down at himself, he realized that no one would take his scruffy appearance for that of a duke. He experienced an almost uncontrollable urge to laugh. "Yes," was all he could say. They were his gardens, after all. And he did design them and work in them. So in a sense, he *was* the gardener.

"Well, you still might try to watch where you are going next time," the girl said. By God, she was looking him straight in the eye and truly believed he was the gardener. It was too good. "I am sure you are quite busy and all," she continued, "with such a large estate to care for. But you must know that the duchess has a house full of guests who might be wandering the gardens at any time. You really must be more careful." The petulant tone had disappeared and she seemed less offended. Interesting. He would have expected most young women of her station—for she must be aristocratic to have been invited by his mother—to disdain the working staff. He would have expected her to rail against his clumsiness, to threaten to report him to his employer, to exert all the superiority of her station. Instead, she looked wistfully down at the crushed blossom in her palm.

"And I was not picking your flowers, if you must know," she continued. "I was simply admiring them. I must have accidentally grabbed at it when you fell over me."

"Yes. Yes, of course," Stephen muttered. His cheeks felt warm and he knew he must be blushing as he recalled how he had been sprawled atop her. "I should not have shouted at you. It is just that . . ." He paused and looked down at the remains of the tiny purple flower. "Well, you cannot know how precious that little plant is."

"Oh, but I can," she replied. "It is a pure *viola odorata*, is it not?"

"Why, yes," he said, completely taken aback that this young girl would know such a thing. "Yes, it is. How did you know?"

"Oh, I have never actually seen one before," she said, "not really, anyway. But I have seen many pictures of them. I love flowers, you see and have—had—many books on the subject. Some with lovely colored prints of various blossoms. Violets have always been my favorites, the simple *viola odorata* most of all. When I saw this patch of them," she said, gesturing to the clump of purple blossoms at the edge of the path, "I could not resist examining them up close. You must have cultivated them especially to bloom so long into summer, did you not? I thought to sketch one, you see. Oh, and I had also considered drawing this one, too," she added, bending to admire the fringed gentian. "Very unusual. The dark blue color-

ing and the fringed edges are a combination I have
never before seen. Are they a special hybrid?"

Stephen's breath was almost knocked out of him as
he listened to this extraordinary speech. Here was a
very pretty young girl, with dark blond curls spilling
out of her bonnet and huge gray eyes peering at him
guilelessly, who knew about rare flowers and special
hybrids—his favorite subjects—and wasn't fawning
all over him. And she actually had no idea who he
was.

It was delicious.

It was too perfect.

He could not keep from smiling.

"Yes," he said at last. "How clever of you to notice.
They are indeed a special hybrid. I developed the
strain myself."

"How wonderful," she exclaimed. "You must be
very proud. Of everything here at Chissingworth."

"I am indeed," he said, strangely affected by her
genuine interest and admiration for the one thing in
his life of which he was truly proud. "You must feel
free to sketch or paint all you want while at Chissingworth," he said. "I promise you will not be so rudely
accosted again."

She smiled at him, and he almost forgot to breathe.
"Thank you," she said. "I imagine there are many
other rare specimens besides *viola odorata*. It would be
lovely to sketch them."

"I would be pleased to show you the gardens myself, and point out the most unusual specimens and
such." He could have bitten his tongue off the moment the words were spoken. What on earth had
made him say such a thing? He was trying to hide
from his mother's guests. He had no business encouraging this young girl, this very pretty young girl, to
fraternize with him. What if she discovered his true
identity?"

"How kind of you," she said, flashing a brilliant

smile. "I would enjoy that. What better tour guide could I possibly ask for than Chissingworth's gardener? By the way," she said, "I am Miss Catherine Forsythe."

Good Lord. What was he to do now? Introduce himself as the owner of Chissingworth, not merely the gardener? How would she treat him, then? Her open, artless conversation would change to egregious fawning and preening, and that inevitable predatory glint would brighten her eyes. He did not believe he could bear it.

And so, how should he introduce himself? Give his name as Stephen Archibald Frederick Charles Godfrey Manwaring? Would she recognize that moniker as belonging to the Duke of Carlisle?

Perhaps not. Perhaps if he just shortened it, did not give her all the important bits, he might get away with it. "I am Stephen Archibald," he blurted, without further thought.

"I am pleased to meet you, Mr. Archibald," she said.

By God, it had worked. She believed it. Miss Forsythe truly believed him to be Mr. Archibald, the gardener at Chissingworth. He bit back a grin. It was almost too perfect.

"And I must tell you how much I have enjoyed your gardens," she continued. "I have only just arrived, though, and look forward to seeing the rest of the grounds during my stay."

"Shall we meet again tomorrow morning, then?" he asked. "I could show you the botanical gardens where the more exotic plants are kept." It was the least frequented area of the estate and they were unlikely to run into any other wandering guests.

"That would be lovely."

"The same time tomorrow morning, then? But some other place, please. I would not have you reminded of our ignominious introduction here.

Through those hedges and a bit beyond is the Chinese garden. There is a small pavilion in the center. I could meet you there."

"Assuming the duchess or my aunt have no other plans for me," she said, "I shall be there. Thank you so much, Mr. Archibald. I look forward to it."

With a wave and a smile, she was off, disappearing through the entrance to the rose garden. Stephen watched her go and gave a wistful sigh.

And wondered what on earth he had got himself into.

Chapter 5

The rest of Catherine's day was filled with organized activity, and she did not have time to dwell on her remarkable encounter with Chissingworth's gardener. She had been much more interested in the tour of the house led by the duchess. Those guests who had never before visited the famous estate were led from room to room while the duchess provided animated commentary, liberally spiced with family anecdotes. The public rooms and state bedrooms were quite grand, befitting a ducal residence. The family rooms, however—the drawing room, various salons, the library, the breakfast room—were much more informal and comfortable.

Catherine had sent up a silent prayer of thanks that the entire house was not as imposing as the public areas. She did not think she would so much enjoy being a guest if she had been given a state bedroom— imagine sleeping in the Queen's bed!—or spending each day in the formal reception rooms. It was all quite daunting.

Later that afternoon, Molly helped her to dress for dinner, then hurried off to do the same for Susannah. While Catherine put the finishing touches on her coiffure, she was interrupted by a soft knock at the door.

"Come in."

A young maid entered and bobbed a curtsy. "Excuse me, miss," she said as she walked toward the dressing table where Catherine sat. She held out a beautiful posy of violets, gathered together in a tidy mound of blossoms, neatly enclosed in sprigs of greenery, and tied with a pale lavender ribbon. "Compliments of the Chissingworth gardens, miss."

Catherine took the posy and held it to her nose. "Thank you," she said as the little maid bobbed again and left the room. Violets! They were not *viola odorata*, of course. But they were beautiful. She wondered if every female guest was given such a favor and secretly hoped they were not. She suspected they were especially for her, from Mr. Archibald. Perhaps his way of apologizing for knocking her to the ground.

She smiled as she recalled their encounter of that morning. Though somewhat clumsy, he seemed a very nice man. It would be a special treat to have someone so knowledgeable show her about the estate gardens. The errant thought that he was also youngish and rather good-looking was immediately dismissed as irrelevant. She had more important fish to bait and had no business having such thoughts about a common laborer, no matter how green his eyes.

It occurred to her, though, that he could not have been a common laborer after all. Though his appearance was certainly not that of a gentleman—she remembered his dirt-smeared smock and battered straw hat—his speech and manners were refined. She would not have expected a gardener, even the head gardener of an estate as large as Chissingworth, to seem such a gentleman in his manners. He was obviously well educated.

Perhaps he was something more than a gardener. Perhaps he was one of those landscape designers, like Capability Brown or Humphrey Repton. She had once, years ago, had the opportunity to peruse Mr. Repton's book, *Sketches and Hints on Landscape Gardening*. Mr. Repton was obviously a well-educated man. Perhaps Mr. Archibald held a similar occupation; perhaps he was more of a designer than a mere gardener. Such a place as Chissingworth would need the services of a designer to bring all the grounds into harmony. She must remember to ask him tomorrow.

Catherine buried her nose once again in the posy, breathing in the soft, elusive fragrance of the violets. What a kind man he was to send her such an offering. He must have remembered her remark that violets were her favorite flowers. As she held out the posy and ran her fingers over the satin ribbon, she realized the flowers were the perfect complement to the pale blue silk of her gown. Of Miss Fairchild's gown, she should say.

As she pinned the posy to her bodice, she admired Susannah's handiwork in transforming the dress by the simple addition of embroidered ribbon trim and a new flounce. Miss Fairchild would never recognize it as having once belonged to her.

The violets were the perfect accessory, and so there was no need to avail herself of any of the more grand pieces of jewelry procured by MacDougal. She was still a bit nervous about wearing some of the finer pieces, in any case. But there was a simple, delicate amethyst pendant on a gold chain which would be just the thing. Simple and inconspicuous, yet of a quality that would not embarrass her among such lofty guests as were gathered at Chissingworth.

When Susannah and Aunt Hetty came to collect her for dinner, Catherine was confident that she did not appear the least bit shabby genteel. And, of course, Susannah looked gorgeous. But then, her beautiful sister would look stunning in sackcloth.

As they descended the stairs three abreast, Catherine was asked about her violets. She gave them a spirited account of her encounter with Mr. Archibald, so that all three ladies were delightfully flushed with laughter as they approached the drawing room below.

"How extraordinary," Susannah said. "I did not know there were men who actually made a living designing gardens."

Aunt Hetty chuckled. "Did you think gardens just sprang up naturally? Arranged in perfect patterns by nature, simply to be pleasing to our eyes?"

"I suppose I never really thought of it," Susannah replied. "And your Mr. Archibald arranged the gardens here at Chissingworth?"

"Not just the formal gardens but the grounds as well, I should think," Catherine replied.

"What do you mean, the grounds?" Susannah's brow beetled in confusion.

"The trees, the lakes and ponds, the parklands. The whole estate."

Susannah stopped in her tracks and glared at her sister. "But . . . but you cannot design trees and lakes. They are just there where God put them."

Aunt Hetty chuckled and patted Susannah's arm. "Not necessarily, my dear," she said. "In most private estates nature has been rearranged to please the eye. The trees placed just so, lakes dug or filled in, as required to achieve the proper effect. Landscapes are often designed in much the way you would design a dress, to please the eye, to accommodate the latest fashion, that sort of thing."

Susannah stared openmouthed at Aunt Hetty, as if she had just uttered some arcane blasphemy. She turned her huge blue eyes upon Catherine, as if seeking confirmation. "Is that true, Cath? All those beautiful trees and creeks and such we saw as we came through Chissingworth were all designed to be that way? By your Mr. Archibald?"

"Or someone before him, I should think. The plantings are not recent." Catherine tugged her sister along once again toward the drawing room.

"My goodness!" Susannah exclaimed. "I had no idea. I assumed everything was just naturally beautiful. Who would have imagined that it was the hand of Man and not the hand of God that created such vistas? My goodness! He must be very clever, this Mr. Archibald, to know how to do all that. I should like to meet him, I think."

"Do not concern yourself with Mr. Archibald, Sukey," Catherine said. "There are more important gentlemen for you to impress this evening." She stopped and turned toward her sister and lowered her voice so that the footmen hovering beside the drawing room doors would not overhear. "We must make certain, Aunt Hetty, that the duchess introduces us to Lord Warburton. His father is an earl and he has an income and estate of his own through his grandmother."

Her aunt quirked a brow at such intelligence. "MacDougal," Catherine whispered, and her aunt nodded in understanding. Turning back toward her sister, she knotted her brows in earnest. "Sukey," she began, "you must remember to be very pleasant to Lord Warburton. He is eminently eligible. You may also allow Mr. Percival Brooke—you recall meeting him this afternoon?—to engage your attention. He has no title, but is the grandson of an earl and extremely rich. You must be cautiously civil to all other unmarried gentlemen until we know their circumstances." She glared at her sister, dismayed at the all-too-familiar look of wide-eyed apprehension. Too many such instructions would only confuse Susannah. The resulting nervousness coupled with her nearsightedness could result in disaster.

"Do not worry, Sukey," Catherine said, patting her sister's hand. "You look beautiful and everyone will love you. Just try to remember about Lord Warburton and Mr. Brooke."

Susannah gave a tremulous smile. "I will *try* to remember, Cath. Really, I will. But there are *so* many people here. I will just have to make a special effort to remember those two gentlemen. Mr. Warburton and Lord Brooke."

Catherine sighed in exasperation. "*Lord* Warburton and *Mr.* Brooke," she said, trying to ignore her aunt's stifled chuckling.

"Oh, yes," Susannah said. "Of course. I have it now."

It was going to be a very long month, Catherine thought as the drawing room doors were opened for them by the footmen.

Stephen arrived twenty minutes early for their appointment. He wondered if Miss Forsythe would come at all. She had not been certain that she would be free, after all. Stephen decided it did not matter if she did not come. He should not expect it. In fact, he should rather be hoping she would not come, for it was sheer lunacy to arrange a meeting with one of his mother's guests. What on earth had possessed him?

He puttered around the Chinese garden as if he had no other occupation in mind. He plucked away dead columbine blossoms, reminding himself that they must be cut back within the month, and trimmed a few wayward branches of honeysuckle. The bamboo plants near the small, slope-roofed pavilion had become overgrown. He must have them thinned.

"Good morning!"

Stephen looked up at the sound of her voice. Miss Forsythe stood on the red-painted bridge—a bit of folly he now thought of as embarrassingly trite—and waved at him. She lifted her skirts slightly as she descended the bridge, providing him a fleeting glimpse of very trim ankles. She flashed a brilliant smile as she walked toward him.

"What a glorious day!" she said. "And what a lovely garden, Mr. Archibald." Her gray eyes darted about, those intriguingly dark brows bobbing up and down with interest. "I have never before seen a Chinese garden. Good heavens. Is that real bamboo?" She strolled toward the pavilion and fingered the spiky leaves, then jumped back and laughed when she discovered they could be very sharp indeed. "I did not know bamboo grew in this country. I remember as a child my mother had a few small pieces of faux bamboo furniture that always intrigued me. I never thought to see the real thing. How wonderful."

Stephen watched her in fascination. She was absolutely delightful, her heart-shaped face animated with eager curiosity. And she looked very pretty this morning in a green muslin gown and matching bonnet. He found himself bursting with unexpected pride as he saw his garden through her eyes.

"Would you like to sketch it?" he asked.

Miss Forsythe looked around the garden and smiled. "The morning light is just about perfect. It is very tempting."

"Oh, but I see you did not bring your drawing materials," he said as he realized he would have expected her to be carrying a large sketchbook and a case of pencils, pastels, and charcoal. Perhaps she had decided to leave that for another day.

Miss Forsythe's hand reached into a pocket, and he could have sworn a brief shadow passed over her eyes. But perhaps it was only a trick of the light. "I have all I need right here," she said, her smile somehow less brilliant. "But I think I will wait. I am only going to allow myself one drawing today, and so I will wait for something really special. I would much prefer to spend the time touring the grounds with you. I have been so excited to know that I am the only one to have such an expert guide."

"Ah," he said. "Then you have not told the other guests of our appointment?"

"Of course not!" she said, and he expelled a breath he had not know he had been holding. Thank God she had not announced his presence to the entire company. "I am selfishly keeping you all to myself," she added with a grin.

"Shall we walk, then?" he asked.

"Lead on, Mr. Archibald."

And so she still had not discovered his true identity. He did not know what perverse pleasure he thought he would enjoy by misleading this innocent young girl. But some imp of mischief urged him on in his deception. She must surely learn who he was eventually. What would she think of him, then?

He led her through the Chinese garden and toward one of the botanical gardens where he kept most of the North American plantings. As they approached the clearing dominated by American plane trees and Canadian red maples, Stephen noticed that two of his workmen were attending to a new planting of black locust. *Oh, Lord.* He must get them out of there before they gave him away.

"Excuse me, Miss Forsythe," he said as he dashed ahead to speak to the men.

"I have a guest to view the botanical gardens," he told the workmen, who had stood and doffed their caps when they first saw him. "Please leave us," he said in a lowered voice. "You can attend to this when we are through. I should think an hour would be sufficient." He sensed Miss Forsythe had approached from behind, and his stomach seized up in knots.

"Yes, Your Gr—"

"That will be all, Tomkins," Stephen interrupted. "Thank you."

"Yes, Your Gr—"

"Thank you. You may go now." The two men stared at him wide-eyed, but nodded, gathered their tools, and left. Stephen almost collapsed with relief. He took a deep breath and blew it out through puffed cheeks. He then turned to face Miss Forsythe, indicating with a sweep of his arm that she should enter the garden.

"I had wondered," she said as her eyes followed the retreating workmen, "if you were not the head gardener. You spoke yesterday with such possessiveness about the grounds that I thought you must be. But then I considered that you might instead be some sort of landscape designer. Like Mr. Humphrey Repton."

"Repton! Please, Miss Forsythe, do not equate me with that arrogant peacock. His work is all artifice and no science." The girl looked distressed at his outburst, and so he smiled down at her to take the sting out of his words. "I beg your pardon, ma'am, for my harsh reaction, but I am afraid you hit upon a sensitive subject with me. Repton actually came here once—uninvited, I might add—to view the grounds. He had the audacity to advise me on the disposition of trees." Stephen chuckled as he recalled his one and only meeting with Repton, who had come hoping to commission a Red Book for Chissingworth, and had expected one and all to kowtow in admiration.

"I gather, then, that you are not an advocate of the picturesque?" Miss Forsythe said.

"I confess I have not the least understanding of it. It seems so much silliness to me. But then, I suppose I am nothing more than an ordinary gardener—a botanist, actually—and will never see the sense in all those artificial vistas. Do you know," he continued, chuckling, "that Repton actually suggested I have a few woodsman's cottages built at the far edge of the estate. No woodsmen would live there, mind you. They would be purely decorative structures. He went on to recommend that the cottages, though unoccupied, should have fires lit to allow 'curls of smoke to enliven the landscape.'" Stephen laughed at the recollection and was pleased to hear Miss Forsythe's laughter joining his.

"I suspect," she said, "he only meant to bring to life Wordsworth's words. 'Wreaths of smoke, sent up in silence from among the tress.'"

"Precisely," Stephen said. "Can you imagine anything more ridiculous? But, forgive me, perhaps you are a proponent of the picturesque yourself. I should not speak so disparagingly of what so many others admire. But you asked if I was a landscape designer. You may label me such, if you like, for I do most of the planning here."

"I thought as much," Miss Forsythe said.

"But I much prefer the humbler title of gardener, if the truth be known."

"Ah, but there is nothing at all humble about Chissingworth's gardens, is there? It is a most extraordinary and magical place, due in great part, I should imagine, to your efforts, Mr. Archibald."

She favored him with a smile warm enough to sprout daisies in winter. Stephen's heart tumbled over in his chest at her obvious admiration. He felt uncharacteristically puffed up with his own consequence. And she did not even know he was the duke!

He walked her through the gardens with renewed pride and pointed out several of the more unusual shrubs and trees. Miss Forsythe's genuine interest and intelligent questioning brought an additional spark to the already brilliant morning. Stephen could not remember when he had so enjoyed himself.

She asked to pause for a moment while they admired one of the magnolia trees. She was thoroughly captivated and wished to sketch it.

"You ought to see it in the spring when it is in bloom," he told her.

"I would love to," she said. "But even now it is lovely and quite unlike anything I have seen. Almost tropical."

She seated herself on a nearby rustic bench and pulled out of her pocket a slightly rumpled piece of foolscap and a stubby, blunt pencil. Without hesitation, she began to draw. With such poor tools, Stephen was astonished at the resulting clarity and detail of the sketch.

"You are very talented," he said as he watched her pencil fly across the paper. "I cannot imagine what wonders you could create with good parchment and paints."

"How I wish I had them," she said absently, her gaze lingering on the tree for a moment before resuming the sketch "It has been years since I could afford them, I am afraid."

Her offhand remark stunned him. So, Miss Forsythe was not the coddled, spoiled rich girl he had imagined. No wonder she was so unaffected. Where had his mother found her, then? Perhaps she was some other guest's poor relation who had been allowed to tag along.

This train of thought was interrupted when she spoke again. "I find myself fascinated by so many foreign plants," she said without looking up. Stephen's eyes were drawn back to her sketch, and he became almost spellbound as he watched the magnolia tree magically take shape on the rumpled foolscap, its glossy, dark leaves seeming to shine on the page. "There are many plants here I have only read about," she continued. "It is really quite a marvelous collection. How did you come by all these American plants?

"Some came by way of Kew, courtesy of Sir Joseph Banks," he said as he watched her add just the right amount of shadow so that the waxy leaves seemed to glow on the page. "The others I collected in my travels with John Fraser."

She looked up with a start. "You have traveled to America?"

Good God. He had been so transfixed by her work he had forgot his imposture for a moment and spoke to her as the duke. Where was his brain? "I, um, was allowed the trip as a part of my education as a young man. I was, um, very fortunate to have such an opportunity."

And so he was. If his father had been alive, he would no doubt have sent Stephen off on the typical Grand Tour once he was finished at university. Instead, he had tramped all over North America with Fraser, collecting plant specimens. It had been sometimes rough and not at all romantic, but it had been the most wonderful experience of his life. There were *some* advantages to being a duke, after all. He could come and go as he pleased.

"How wonderful," Miss Forsythe said, returning her attention to the drawing. "I suppose the Duke of Carlisle arranged it for you?"

"It was at the duke's expense, yes," Stephen said, biting back a smile. "His Grace has been very generous."

"How lucky you are," she continued.

"Indeed," he said. Even at this very moment, he was thanking his stars that he had been able to maintain this idiotic charade for one more day. And wondering how much longer his luck would last.

Chapter 6

Catherine saw the objects the moment she opened her eyes the next morning. Piled atop the window bench were a stack of drawing pads, sheets and sheets of parchment, and a low wooden case that looked for all the world like the paintbox she had once owned as a young girl. She rubbed her eyes, thinking she must be dreaming; but when she looked again, the paintbox and papers were still there.

She threw the covers aside and bounded, barefoot, to the window bench, tossing the curtains open to allow more light into the room. She ran her fingers delicately over a sheet of parchment, and a shiver of excitement danced down her spine. She never thought to have such good materials again.

But where had they come from?

Knowing that she should leave everything untouched until she had discovered to whom they belonged, Catherine gave in to her curiosity and opened the lid of the wooden case. She gasped with delight at what she found inside: tiny jars of paint in more pigments than she had ever before seen, gum arabic, two small water glasses, several small ivory palettes, and a collection of brushes of all sizes. She picked up one of the brushes ever so carefully, still uncertain if she had any right to touch them at all. This one was a very fine brush, perfect for painting the delicate veins of leaves and flowers. How her fingers itched to do just that.

Catherine was so absorbed in examining the paintbox that she all but ignored the familiar soft knock on the door and the subsequent entry of Molly.

"Good morning, Miss Catherine," Molly said in her normal cheerful tone. "I've brung your chocolate."

"Catherine looked briefly toward the young maid. "Thank you," she said and turned at once back to the paintbox. But something noticed out of the corner of her eye caused her head to whip back around. "Are those violets?" she asked, eying the tiny tussy-mussy perched on the tray.

"Yes, miss. Sweet violets, I think. Cook said I was to bring 'em to you with the chocolate. There's a note, too."

Catherine walked over to the bedside table where Molly had placed the tray and retrieved the folded note. "Compliments of the Chissingworth gardens," it read. There was no signature. Catherine smiled as she picked up the tussy-mussy and brought it to her nose. How very thoughtful of him, she thought as she inhaled the delicate fragrance of the violets; for they could only have come from Mr. Archibald. It had become clear that no other female guest received such favors from the gardens. It made her feel singularly important, somehow. And strangely warm all over as she brought to mind an image of his green eyes smiling down at her. And the easy grin that had so surprised her. He had seemed so dour at first. And yet now, memory of that grin, lopsided and almost boyish, gave her an odd tremor of anticipation.

Would she see him again today?

It was strange how much she looked forward to their strolls together. He was only the gardener, after all. But he was so easy to talk to. She could be quite comfortable with him. She often found herself speaking openly and candidly with him about almost any subject that arose. Only yesterday she had hinted to him of her poverty without the slightest qualm about doing so. It was his position, she supposed, that inspired such ease. Every other person at Chissingworth was her social superior. When she was with Mr. Archibald, she did not have to worry about making an impression, about disguising her circumstances.

Given a choice, Catherine would rather stroll about the gardens with the knowledgeable guidance of the head gardener than the effusive chatter of Sir Bertram Fanshawe or one of the other gentlemen guests. The fact that the gardener was infinitely more attractive than any other man at Chissingworth had nothing to do with it.

The sound of Molly opening the bedchamber door interrupted Catherine's thoughts. She did not want the girl to leave before questioning her about the paints, for she suspected Molly's uncle was somehow behind their unexpected appearance. "Just a moment, Molly. Do you happen to know what these are doing in my bedchamber?" she asked, a sweep of her arm indicating the paintbox and papers on the window bench.

"Oh yes, miss. I brung 'em in whilst you were still sleepin'. I tried not to wake you."

"But where did you get them?"

"One of the chambermaids give 'em to me and says Mrs. Beddowes told her I was to give 'em to you. I hope I did right," Molly added with wide-eyed apprehension.

"You are certain they were meant for me?"

"Oh yes, miss. Mrs. Beddowes told the chambermaid to make sure as Miss Catherine Forsythe received 'em. Clear as day, she was. Miss Catherine Forsythe, she said."

"Well," Catherine said, smiling as she picked up one of the brushes again and touched its soft bristles with the tip of a finger. "How very kind. I suppose MacDougal must have mentioned how much I enjoy painting."

"I'm sure I don't know, miss. I ain't . . . that is, I haven't seen Uncle Thomas all morning."

"It does not matter," Catherine said absently, her thoughts on all the beautiful specimens in the gardens just waiting for her paintbrush. "But please thank Mrs. Beddowes for me. And I shall do the same when next I see her."

Catherine wanted nothing else but to sit down that very moment and begin painting. It had been so long since she had had paints that her hands almost shook with excitement. But she knew she must get dressed and join the others for breakfast. She walked over and picked up the cup of chocolate. As she sipped it, she tried to recall the plans for today, wondering if and when she might find time to sneak away to the gardens with her new paintbox. Her glance strayed once again to the tussy-mussy of violets. She smiled as an idea struck her. She picked up the flowers and carried them over to the small writing desk near the window.

Sometime later, Molly returned and was aghast to find that Catherine had neither washed nor dressed. She quickly helped Catherine to do both. Molly apologized profusely for the cold temperature of the wash water, when it was Catherine's fault that it had been allowed to cool, and for the simple chignon she was forced to fashion with so little time. The rushed toilette would have to do.

Adjusting the pins in her hair, Catherine dashed down the long corridor with very unladylike speed and practically bounded down the stairs. When she reached the breakfast room, most of the guests had already left, but there were still a few stragglers, so she did not feel utterly gauche for being so late. Two of those lingering over their coffee were Susannah and Aunt Hetty. Catherine filled a plate from the sideboard and joined them.

After only a few words of greeting, they were joined by Lord Strickland. Both Forsythe sisters had been introduced to the earl the previous evening. Catherine had quickly divined that he was unmarried and mentally added him to her list of potential husbands. His joining them at breakfast meant that Susannah had no doubt caught his eye, and that, at least, was a good sign. He was attractive, with dark hair and eyes, and a pleasing smile. Unlike some of the other gentlemen in attendance, Lord Strickland did not seem the least bit frivolous. On the contrary, he had an aura of seriousness about him that hinted at solid dependability.

He would do very nicely, Catherine thought, so long as his circumstances were acceptable. She would have to ask MacDougal to investigate. She thought of the paintbox again and wondered what they would do without their invaluable manservant.

"And what have you ladies planned for this morning?" Lord Strickland asked, his eyes sweeping all three of them but resting on Susannah at last.

"Lady Raymond and a few others have organized an outing to the village," Susannah answered in her breathiest voice. "They have asked me to join them." She sounded utterly surprised that anyone would wish for her company.

"And you, Mrs. Hathaway?" the earl asked, turning to Aunt Hetty. "Are you driving into the village as well?"

Aunt Hetty chuckled. "No, no," she said. "I shall leave that to the young people. I will stay here and have a nice quiet coze with some of the other older women."

"And you, Miss Catherine? What are your plans?"

Catherine thought of the paintbox and dismissed all notions of a village outing. "Frankly, I had thought to explore the gardens a bit more. They are so lovely. And so vast, I have not seen even half, I am sure."

"Have you seen the Italian garden?" he asked.

"I do not believe so."

"Then perhaps you will allow me to be your guide," Lord Strickland said. "It is one of my favorites of all the Chissingworth gardens. I would be honored if you would join me in a walk there."

Catherine was momentarily discomposed that the earl should be seeking her company and not that of her beautiful sister. It was unexpected, but very gratifying. She smiled and accepted his offer.

Less than an hour later, she strolled alongside Lord Strickland through the familiar gardens nearest the house. After a time, they finally cut off toward the east, a direction she had not yet explored. Flower gardens gave way to shrubbery gardens. They were soon following a gravel path bordered by very tall, neatly clipped hedges. The path curved one way and then another, so that she could not really see where they were going.

"This is known as the Serpentine Walk, for obvious reasons," the earl told her. "It allows an element of surprise when we finally reach our destination.

When the walk at last opened up quite unexpectedly onto a large formal garden, Catherine did indeed gasp in surprise. "How wonderful!" she exclaimed.

"Welcome to the Italian garden," the earl said with a smile.

The huge expanse of garden was ringed by a fine bank of arbutus, laurustinus, and other evergreens. A network of gravel walks bordered by ornamental shrubbery all met in the center at a large marble fountain supported by the figures of four dolphins. At one end of the garden, orange trees in wooden tubs were arranged in front of a building that boasted a series of large paned windows across the entire front.

"That is the old orangery," Lord Strickland said. "I believe it was built in the last century by the present duke's grandfather."

At the opposite end was a terrace ascended by a series of diagonal balustraded slopes. In the center of the balustrade along the top stood a huge classical statue flanked by two smaller statues. Other classical sculpture dotted the garden.

"The present duke's father had this garden built to display his collection of Roman sculpture, acquired during his Grand Tour." Lord Strickland's gaze swept the garden from end to end. He turned to Catherine and smiled. "I have always been pleased that Carlisle has chosen to leave it intact. Though he has put in a new orangery and is even now building a modern conservatory, he had shown good sense in allowing some of these older, less fashionable settings to remain unchanged."

"You seem to know quite a lot about Chissingworth, my lord," Catherine said. "Have you visited often?"

"Quite often. The duke and I have been friends for years, you see. I have spent many a summer among these gardens."

"And where is the duke this summer?" Catherine asked. She thought she saw a flicker of apprehension cross the earl's face before he replied.

"I . . . I could not say. He does not enjoy his mother's parties. He generally takes care to be away during such occasions. Here, let me show you these agave plants."

Catherine could sense that the topic of the duke was an uncomfortable one for Lord Strickland, and so she let it drop. No doubt he did not wish to admit that the man was simply unfit to take part in a social gathering. She admired his sensitivity and loyalty toward his friend, which only served to increase his eligibility

in Catherine's eyes. Such a man would make a wonderful husband for Susannah. She followed the earl
toward one of several huge spiky plants in stone tubs,
dismissing all thoughts of the absent duke in favor of
the more interesting subject of exotic plants.

Stephen was inordinately happy to see Miss
Forsythe perched in front of a patch of white bryony,
sketchpad on her lap and paintbox open on the bench
next to her. He halfway looked for her every time he
wandered through the gardens, but always per-
suaded himself that he would not be disappointed if
he did not see her every day. But the sight of her this
afternoon bent over the sketchpad made him smile
with anticipation.

Not wanting to startle her and perhaps ruin her
painting, he waited until she had finished tracing a
delicate outline of leaf and pulled the brush away
from the page. Before she could dip again into the
glass of water, he cleared his throat. She turned
around at the sound. When she saw him, her face lit
up with a smile that singed him to his toes.

"Hello!" she cried, a look of pure delight in her
eyes.

By God, she was happy to see him. Not His Grace,
but plain Mr. Archibald. He could not say that he had
ever experienced such unbiased regard, and his heart
swelled with pleasure.

"Look!" she said, her face as animated as a child's
at Christmas. "See what I have!"

"Aha," he said as he moved closer. "You have
found painting materials. How fortunate for you."

"Yes, it certainly is," she said with breathless enthusiasm. "I cannot tell you when I have been so excited.
It has been donkey's years since I have had a real
paintbox. And such colors! Carmine, vermilion,
Prussian blue, even ultramarine. Is it not wonderful?"

"Indeed." Stephen had remembered the paints and

brushes and drawing materials and such up in the old schoolroom. He had never shown any talent with them as a boy, and so they had languished unused for years. He had asked Mrs. Beddowes to locate them and make them available to Miss Forsythe. He was a man of great fortune and had often used it generously to help others, or simply to give someone pleasure. But rarely in all his life had anyone so appreciated one of his gifts. And such a simple offering that had cost him nothing at all. How curious. And how curiously satisfying.

"I have no idea where they came from," she continued, "though I have my suspicions. My maid insists that Mrs. Beddowes meant them for me and so I shall not protest. I have hardly been able to contain myself until I could get away this afternoon and bring them into the garden. Oh!" Her smile brightened, if that was possible. "I have something for you."

For *him?* She had something for *him?* She had no idea he was responsible for the paints, and yet she had something for him?

Miss Forsythe briefly rifled through the sheets of parchment and pulled out a painted page. "Here," she said as she held it out to him. "I wanted you to know how much I appreciate the posies of violets. No, do not deny it," she said, raising a hand as he started to speak. "I know it is you who is responsible for providing them. And I thank you for it. They are my favorite flower, as I believe I told you. As a small token of my thanks, I made this for you."

The parchment sheet was painted with a few violets and leaves, not the whole bouquet, but just a sample specimen. It was an impressively accurate picture, capturing both the range of shadings of the flower petals as well as their delicate porcelain texture.

"You painted this for me?" he asked, studying the picture. "But this is excellent. Truly excellent." He looked up to see a faint blush coloring her cheeks.

"Do you really think so?" she asked in a suddenly shy voice.

He did. Stephen was more than a little familiar with botanical illustration. His vast library included the complete works of Redouté as well as several earlier painters. He knew Miss Forsythe to be talented with a pencil. But he had never expected her paintings to be so fine. Many society ladies these days had taken up the art of flower painting, reducing it to a genteel accomplishment. But here was no trivial exercise. There was nothing mawkish or sentimental about it. Miss Forsythe's painting was bold and exactly observed, beautifully and skillfully executed.

"I do indeed," he replied. "You are very talented, Miss Forsythe."

She blushed to the roots of her hair and dropped her gaze to her lap. "Thank you, Mr. Archibald. You are very kind to say so."

"Not at all. And I thank you for the wonderful picture." The words sounded empty when measured against the swell of emotion in his breast. She had given him, freely, something of herself, and made especially for him by her own hand. He could not have treasured it more if it had been the rarest of West Indian black orchids. He swallowed heavily against the strange lump in his throat.

"I am so glad you like it," she said. "I hoped you would, for I so appreciate the flowers you have sent to me." She laughed and quirked a brow as she looked up at him. "At first I thought that perhaps all the female guests received such tokens, 'compliments of the Chissingworth gardens.' But I soon discovered that I was the only one so well favored. I will admit to you that I have often felt inadequate here at Chissingworth among such fine company. My sister and I do not normally move in such circles. Ha! We do not normally move in *any* circles. In any case, being singled out as the only recipient of Chissingworth violets has made me feel very special indeed. Thank you so much, Mr. Archibald."

Her warm smile made *him* feel very special indeed. Not because he was one of the highest peers in the land, but because she thought he was quite the opposite and liked him anyway.

It pained him to consider what she may think of him once she discovered his deception.

Later that evening, as he tried to work in his office off the old conservatory, he was constantly distracted by thoughts of Miss Forsythe, by images of her dancing gray eyes and those magnificent, dark, animated brows. He wondered who she was and how his mother had managed to include her among the guests. If the girl was as ill circumstanced as she implied, he could not imagine the duchess condescending to associate with her. Perhaps he should ask his mother.

But, no, that would not do. If Stephen so much as hinted at an interest in a woman, his mother would start fussing and scheming and causing all sorts of trouble. Besides, how could he explain that he was interested in a woman who thought him the gardener? Even the head gardener? The duchess would never understand. He did not understand it himself. Was he, in fact, 'interested'?

All his adult life, he had avoided Society women, even those on the fringes, as appeared to be the case with Miss Forsythe. The moment they were presented to His Grace the Duke of Carlisle, their interest became decidedly predatory. Though at two-and-thirty he should be expected to marry and set up his nursery, he had no intention of doing so. Let his cousin Henry inherit. Stephen had no wish to be saddled for life with a woman who cared only for his rank and fortune. As he suspected his father had been.

And, of course, the reason Miss Forsythe so intrigued him—well, one of the reasons, anyway—was that she seemed to like him for himself. She was the first and only woman in his entire life about whom he could honestly say that.

But how much longer could he keep his true identity secret? Twice now he had been forced to interrupt staff gardeners before they could address him as "Your Grace" in Miss Forsythe's presence. She must think him an insufferable bully with his workmen. Once, as they strolled about the gardens chatting comfortably about this and that, she had mentioned her impressions of the house and its grandeur. "The duchess," she had said, "gave some of us a tour of the house. She mentioned there are over one hundred and fifty rooms at Chissingworth. Can you imagine? One hundred and fifty rooms?"

"One hundred and seventy-eight, actually," he had responded without thinking. "There are fifty-four large rooms—salons, reception rooms, dining rooms, and the like. Ninety-six bedchambers and dressing rooms. Three kitchens. Eighteen assorted offices and workshops. None of that includes the servants' quarters, some of which are not in the main house itself. I've forgot how many rooms they occupy, but at last count there were eighty-seven house servants. Another twenty-three work the stables, and thirty-five tend the gardens."

Miss Forsythe had stared at him openmouthed, and he suddenly realized that he had been blithely spouting off statistics that were second nature to him. "Good heavens," she had said at last, "it is almost like its own small community, is it not? You know Chissingworth well, Mr. Archibald. You must have spent many years employed here."

"I have lived here my whole life," he told her. "As did my father and his before him."

He volunteered no more information and steered the conversation toward more prudent subjects. It was clear she simply assumed that he was the product of succeeding generations of Chissingworth gardeners. She never questioned his knowledge of the place and never suspected he was its owner. But how much longer could he sustain this ridiculous pretense?

He did not like to think how their budding friendship would change once she realized who he was. Would her open, unaffected, sweet manner turn into obsequious fawning? He did not like to think so. He preferred to think of her as completely unspoiled, though he realized she was probably no such thing. Nevertheless, he intended to keep his illusions intact for the time being.

With a sweep of his arm, he brushed aside the assorted clutter on his desk and propped up Miss Forsythe's painting against a stack of books. There. Now he could admire it while he worked. In the next breath, however, it slid down flat upon the desk. *Damn.* Reaching into a drawer, he pulled out a handful of tacks, but looking around the room, he could find no hammer. Without further thought, he bent down and began unlacing his boot, then tugged and tugged until it was free. Using the heel of his work boot, he tacked the picture to the edge of the bookcase above his desk.

"A new addition to your collection, Carlisle?"

Stephen turned to see a grinning Miles standing in the doorway. "Well, come on in, old chap. Clear off a chair and have a seat. And yes, this one is new. It's quite a good one, don't you think?"

Miles bent over the desk to peer at the picture. "Yes. Very nice. Violets, eh? Very nice." He turned to locate a chair, removed a stack of journals from one, and sat down.

Stephen reached in a lower desk drawer and brought out a silver flask and two drinking glasses. After pouring each of them a finger or two of whiskey, he settled back in his chair and crossed his stockinged foot over his booted one. "And so, how goes the search, Miles? Any prime candidates among mother's guests?"

"Several, actually." Miles grinned, then took a swallow of whiskey. "You might want to reconsider your commitment to stay away."

Stephen laughed. "Not a chance. But tell me about the young ladies, anyway."

"Well, let's see. There is Miss Phillipina Cummings."

"Sherrington's daughter?"

"Yes, that's right. Very pretty, very energetic, and very young." Miles took another sip of whiskey. "Lady Alice Landridge is here. A trifle forward for my taste. Oh, and speaking of which, Sophia Onslow is here."

"Lady Onslow? The merry widow? You had better watch your step with that one, my friend."

"Don't worry, I will," Miles replied in perfect seriousness. "But, to continue. There is Miss Fenton-Sykes, red-haired and full of life. And Lady Rosalind Farnsworth, a raven-haired beauty. Oh, but the real beauty is Miss Forsythe." Stephen almost choked on his whiskey. "She is the most exquisite thing you have ever seen, Stephen. Pale, cornsilk blond hair and enormous blue eyes. Flawless skin. Perfect features. She almost appears to be not of this earth, she is so ethereal and graceful."

Stephen did not recognize this creature as his Miss Forsythe. She was very pretty, to be sure, but there was nothing particularly ethereal about her. On the contrary, she seemed fresh and real and delightfully earthbound. Could she appear so different in Society? Compelled to offer some remark, he said, "She sounds a paragon, Miles. When shall I wish you happy?"

Miles chuckled softly. "Stephen, you know I am not one to move so quickly on such a momentous decision. In any case, the heavenly creature is not for me. She is a bit too . . . too breathless and . . . well, empty-headed. I suspect her sister holds claim to all the sense in the family. Now, *she* just might be a serious contender."

"The sister?" *Ah*. Now he began to understand.

"Yes. Miss Catherine Forsythe. Very pretty, though she has not the staggering beauty of her sister. She seems very bright and quite . . . well, quite innocent and unaffected."

Stephen smiled to think that even in Society, *his* Miss Forsythe maintained her open, unpretentious charm. He expected no less from her, for he was beginning to think her just about perfect.

"And," Miles continued with a sheepish grin, "she seems to like me."

Not quite perfect, then, Stephen thought with uncharacteristic jealousy.

Chapter 7

By the next day, it seemed all the expected guests had arrived, and Catherine was astonished to find that their numbers now surpassed sixty. Imagine such a house, that could comfortably lodge so large a crowd! From bits of overheard conversation she discerned that even husbands and wives were given separate accommodations. The sheer size of the place simply boggled the mind.

And yet, nothing could have better served Catherine's plans. The very fact that the house could so easily entertain such numbers meant a wider selection of prospects for the Forsythe sisters. Surely one of the many gentlemen—or perhaps even two—could be brought up to scratch.

That evening, as the ladies followed the duchess from the dining room, Catherine hurried to catch up with Susannah, who had been seated at the opposite end of the immense table that comfortably seated the entire party. The room itself—once an Elizabethan banqueting hall with its elaborate double hammer-beam roof still intact—was also enormous. Everything about Chissingworth was enormous. How were they ever to return to the tiny, cramped row house in Chelsea after such a place as this?

Catherine was jostled about by the boisterous herd of females and became hopelessly separated from Susannah just when she most wanted to have a word with her. Two dozen and more chattering women nudged her along up the great staircase and toward the Apollo Salon.

It seemed every room at Chissingworth had a special name. With so many rooms it was no doubt the only way of identifying one salon from the next, one sitting room from the next. Catherine had been astonished when she had first seen the Apollo Salon on her tour with the duchess that first day. It was a large drawing room, entirely painted from ceiling to floor with scenes from the life of Apollo. The ceiling itself depicted the birth of Apollo, and around the walls were scenes from his childhood, the foundation of Delphi, his various exploits—amorous and otherwise—as well as his servitude in the pastures of Mount Ida. Not a square inch had been left unpainted by the Italian master Antonio Verrio in the seventeenth century. Larger than life figures seemed to float down from the ceiling and step right out from the walls to dominate the human inhabitants of the room.

As the lively group entered the salon, a shrill voice rose above the din. "Good Lord, Isabelle! How do you manage to live with all these gods and goddesses disporting themselves so . . . so enthusiastically? How is one supposed to carry on a sedate conversation with all these naked bodies constantly drawing the eye. It is quite discomposing."

Shrieks of laughter rang out from the group and the duchess's reply was lost. A plump, middle-aged woman at Catherine's elbow caught her eye and grinned. "Leave it to Leticia Malmsbury to get straight to the point," she said. "Thank goodness Her

Grace is not offended by the tactless old biddy. I cannot imagine why she continues to invite her. I say, are you not one of the Forsythe girls? Sister to that goddess incarnate who has the young men drooling all over their neckcloths?" She chuckled before continuing. "Forgive me. I do not believe we have been introduced. "I am Lady Fairchild."

"I am pleased to make your acquaintance, my lady," Catherine said with a slight curtsy. "I am Miss Catherine Forsythe. And, yes, the goddess is indeed my sister, Susannah." She smiled in the direction of her sister, who had managed to work her way to the opposite corner of the room, and did indeed outshine all the larger-than-life painted goddesses frolicking on the walls and ceiling. She really must speak to her before the gentlemen returned. "I hope you will forgive me, ma'am," Catherine said, "but I must have a quick word with my sister. If you will excuse me . . ."

"I beg your pardon," Lady Fairchild said as she laid a hand upon Catherine's arm, "but where did you get that dress? I mean to say, who is your modiste? Could it be Madame Michaud on Clifford Street?"

Good Lord. *That* Lady Fairchild. The mother of the girl whose cast-off dress Catherine wore at this very moment. She had been off her guard as she sought out Susannah. Had she paid better attention, she could have avoided the woman altogether and been halfway across the room by now. Her stomach clenched up into a thousand knots as she waited to be exposed as a fraud and a thief.

And so soon! It had only been three days and she was still surveying the land, so to speak. No attachments had yet been formed. It was far too early in the game. Dear God, she thought, do not let my plans come to naught so quickly.

Lady Fairchild glared at her, but Catherine was unable to compose herself enough to stammer more than a few noncommittal syllables.

"I only ask," the woman continued, raking Catherine from head to toe with a critical eye, "because several years ago she made a similar dress for my youngest daughter, Eleanor. A very similar dress. I would be willing to swear it was the exact same green silk, or very like, in any case. Of course, the lace trim at the waist is quite different, and the cording along the shoulders is unlike anything she made for Eleanor . . . in fact, it is really quite striking."

"Thank you," Catherine said, offering a trembly smile to Lady Fairchild and a silent prayer of thanks to the heavens for the talented needle of her sister. And suddenly, she saw a possible way out of this coil. It was devious. It was dishonest. But she had come this far and she could not afford to allow Lady Fairchild to expose her. "But how very odd," she said as she fluffed out her green silk skirt with studied nonchalance. "I was told this dress was a unique design. One of a kind, in fact. How disconcerting to know that your daughter had one so similar."

"Disconcerting, indeed!" Lady Fairchild exclaimed in a disgusted tone. "Why, she told us the same taradiddle. One of a kind, she said. The Gallic hussy! You can be sure I will have a word or two with her when I return to Town. Such people must not be allowed to take advantage of their betters."

"Oh, but I did not mean to imply that it was Madame Michaud who made the dress," Catherine quickly added. Despite her own desperate circumstances, she had no wish to be the cause of a perfectly innocent dressmaker losing her custom. "I only meant that *my* modiste had promised the dress was unique. But she is quite young, you see, and may not have fully developed her own style as yet. She mentioned that she had apprenticed with a famous Mayfair modiste. I confess I cannot recall who it was, but it may well have been your Madame Michaud. The girl may not even realize what a strong influence her for-

mer mistress still has on her own designs. I am sure
any similarity was not deliberate.

Lady Fairchild snorted in derision. "Hmph! I still
think it unconscionable that she would have so bla-
tantly copied Madame Michaud's designs. You can be
sure I will inform Madame of this shameless thievery.
What is the upstart's name?"

"Oh, I really do not think that will be necessary,"
Catherine said in her most persuasive tone. She mar-
veled that her voice sounded so calm when fear of ex-
posure still gripped her and caused her heart to
pound in double time against her ribs. "As I said,"
she continued, "the girl is still young and learning.
Let us give her the benefit of the doubt, Lady
Fairchild. I am sure neither of us wants to see her lose
her business so soon. But I assure you, I will have a
discreet word with her when we return to Town."

"See that you do!" Lady Fairchild heaved a sigh
and gave one last lingering look at Catherine's gown.
"Well, I must say I am glad that I shall not be forced
to find another modiste. Madame Michaud has such a
way with a needle. And so does your girl, if this dress
is any indication. She has done a nice job of it, if only
she will learn not to steal someone else's designs."

Catherine nodded her agreement and quickly made
her escape. Good Lord, but that had been a near
thing. Though she was sure Lady Fairchild had been
put off for the moment, Catherine nevertheless almost
swooned with relief. By the time she had reached Susannah across the room, her racing heart had calmed,
and a feeling of triumph had replaced that momentary surge of fear. By God, she was becoming as wily
as MacDougal himself. Even so, she prayed that the
encounter with Lady Fairchild was the last such she
would have to face during the next few weeks.

"Susannah," she said, bending near her sister's ear,
"could I have a word with you, please?"

Susannah excused herself very prettily to the

Misses Neville and Lady Crisp and took Catherine's arm as they walked aside.

"Now, I want you to pay close attention, Sukey, before the gentlemen return."

Susannah turned her blue eyes on Catherine in rapt attention.

"I want you to make a special point," Catherine said, "to become acquainted with Mr. Septimus Phipps."

"Mr. Phipps?"

"Yes. He was seated next to me at supper. He is a handsome young man and well spoken. But, more important, I discovered he is next in line to inherit his uncle's earldom. The Earl of Whitfield, I believe it is. And the present earl is quite elderly, it seems. Besides which, Mr. Phipps is apparently quite well to grass on his own account."

"And you say he is handsome, too?" Susannah asked.

Catherine chuckled. "Yes, Sukey, he is very nice-looking. I believe you will like him. Please ask the duchess to introduce you."

"All right."

Catherine looked up at the sound of opening doors and loud voices. "The gentlemen have returned," she said. "Oh, and there he is, Sukey. Mr. Phipps. He is the dark-haired gentleman in the bottle green coat."

"Yes. Yes, I see him," Susannah said, squinting toward the doorway as thirty or more gentlemen swarmed into the room, darting off in all directions to capture seats next to their favorite ladies.

Catherine was extraordinarily pleased to see Lord Strickland making his way toward her. Though she was committed to seeing Susannah properly settled, it was gratifying to think that she might have a chance for herself as well. And with an earl, no less.

"Good evening, Miss Forsythe," he said, bowing over her outstretched hand. "With such a crowd, I despaired of finding an opportunity to speak with you. How fortunate that I have found you alone, before all the younger men trip all over themselves to be at your side."

Catherine laughed. "You have me confused with my sister, Lord Strickland. She is the one who commands such attentions, not I."

"But you have my full attention, Miss Forsythe." He offered a warm smile, and Catherine felt a tiny rush of triumph for the second time that evening. All her plans were falling very nicely into place. Even dreams of her own future might well be within reach.

"And I see your sister has commanded Phillips's full attention," he said.

"Mr. Phipps, you mean."

"Septimus Phipps? Good heavens, no. He is over there, fawning all over Miss Fenton-Sykes. She has his full devotion at the moment, I am afraid. No, that is Captain Phillips with your sister."

"Captain Phillips?" Catherine turned around and indeed saw that her sister stood among a circle of eager admirers vying for her attention. And yet she was making calf's eyes at a certain dark-haired gentleman in a bottle green coat.

Blast the girl's nearsightedness, anyway. She had the wrong man!

As the green-coated gentleman turned slightly so that he was facing in Catherine's direction, she saw for the first time that his left sleeve was empty. "Oh, my goodness," she murmured, a hand flying to her mouth.

"Yes, poor Phillips lost an arm at Vitoria," Lord Strickland said, mistaking Catherine's concern. "But at least he came out of it alive. They reduced him to half-pay, of course, poor chap."

A one-armed half-pay officer. *Good Lord.* And Susannah was batting those blue eyes at him for all she was worth, while the very eligible Mr. Phipps was flirting madly with the freckled-face Miss Fenton-Sykes.

How could Susannah have mistaken the one-armed captain for the tall, well-built Mr. Phipps? And once she had discovered who he was, how could she possibly imagine that he was to be considered at all eligible? If the girl had half a brain . . .

Had it been only moments ago that she had been so puffed up with triumph? Catherine stifled a groan.

"Carlisle has been very generous, though," Lord Strickland continued, as though nothing at all were amiss. "They are cousins, you know."

Catherine brightened. "Captain Phillips is cousin to the Duke of Carlisle?"

"On the distaff side of the family, yes. After Vitoria, Carlisle convinced him to sell out and settle here at Chissingworth.""

"Captain Phillips lives here?"

"Yes. He is the steward. Quite a good one, too, I am told. He would have to be, of course. It's a huge estate to manage. It was a wise move on Carlisle's part to put Phillips in charge. Wise as well as generous."

So, he was a steward. A one-armed poor relation of the half-witted Duke of Carlisle employed as a steward. Little more than a glorified servant. A servant with dark hair and a bottle green coat. And Susannah was smiling up at him as though he were the most important man in the world.

Catherine sighed in exasperation and turned her back on the disagreeable scene.

The devil take all beautiful, featherbrained, near-sighted sisters.

"She recognized the dress?"

Miss Forsythe nodded and Stephen burst into laughter.

"There was nothing funny about it, sirrah," she said in a stern tone, belied by the smile she was unable to suppress. "I was terrified that I was about to be found out!"

She turned back to her painting, and Stephen was almost spellbound by the vision of her in the Old Hall garden, the sun behind her inflaming the soft blond curls peeking out from beneath her bonnet. He had an absurd desire to reach out and touch one of those curls. Would it feel as silky as it looked? What he really wanted to do was remove that jaunty little chip straw bonnet and see her hair in all its glory, unpinned and spilling in golden waves down her back. But perhaps her hair was not even long, as he liked to imagine, but cropped fashionably short. The fact that he did not know made him realize he had never seen her without a hat. What would she do if he asked her to remove it?

What would she do if he reached down and kissed her?

But he could not do that. He knew that he could not. But that was all right, for it was pleasure enough just to look at her. For now, it was enough.

If he possessed even half her talent with a paintbrush, he would capture this moment on paper: Miss Forsythe's fair loveliness set off against the remains of the Old Hall, where fountains of clematis sprayed over a ruined wall. Two of the loveliest things he had ever seen.

He had been intrigued by her story of the purloined gowns and silently commended her ingenuity in insuring that she and her sister would be dressed properly while at his mother's party. Entertaining as the tale had been, it still troubled him to think that she should be forced to such measures.

"But you were not found out," he replied at last. "You foiled the dragon before she could strike."

"For the moment," she replied. Looking up from her painting, she cast Stephen a tentative smile. "I discovered a talent for acting I never knew I possessed. It was most exhilarating."

Stephen was momentarily struck by her words. Perhaps she was not quite the artless innocent he had imagined. He decided to probe further.

"Do you mind if I ask you a personal question, Miss Forsythe?"

"That depends upon the question, Mr. Archibald."

"I was just curious about something," he continued. "I gather that you and your sister are not . . . well . . . not terribly secure, financially speaking."

"We are poor as church mice."

"Truly?" She nodded in response and turned her attention back to her painting. "Then, how is it that you came to be invited to Chissingworth in the first place? The duchess is usually very selective in her guests, or so I am told."

"She and my Aunt Hetty were in school together."

"Really?"

"Yes, really." Her eyes were fixed on the tiny ivory palette where she was mixing a shade of reddish purple pigment. "They ran into one another recently after many years, and the duchess kindly invited us. I suspect Aunt Hetty told her the truth of the matter and the duchess, kind lady that she is, saw a way out for Susannah and me and arranged for us to come."

"A way out?" Stephen asked. "How so?"

"By placing us in the company of more than a few unmarried gentlemen, that's how. So that we could find rich husbands."

"Rich husbands?"

"Of course," she said with a momentary lift of a shoulder. She began to fill in a finely outlined clematis blossom with the newly mixed pigment—an astonishingly accurate representation of the unusual color of the tiny flowers that covered the old wall. "In my world," she said, "it is just about the only acceptable avenue of survival for a penniless but well-born young woman. We must marry a fortune."

Stephen flinched at the words "in my world." He had always been impressed with Miss Forsythe's friendly, open manner with a man she considered little more than a gardener. He had taken every advantage of that guileless manner, encouraging her confidence and her trust. Her words just now, though, brought home the fact that she was very much aware of the supposed difference in their stations. His notion of an unspoiled paragon was slowly crumbling at his feet.

"Just before the duchess's invitation arrived," she continued, "I was this close to looking for a position as a teacher or governess. But what on earth could Susannah do? She is too pretty and too scatterbrained to be a governess. She is an excellent seamstress, of course, and probably could have found employment with a dressmaker. But that is a difficult life at best. Susannah is much too delicate for that sort of hardship. I cannot even bear to think of it. So," she added in a lighter tone, "here we are at Chissingworth looking for rich husbands."

Stephen was stunned into silence. He would never in a million years have pegged his guileless Miss Forsythe as a fortune hunter. It went against everything he believed about her. He stared at her in painful disbelief. His silence must have alarmed her, for she turned and looked over her shoulder at him.

"Are you surprised, then?" she asked. "Or perhaps disappointed?"

He did not wish to acknowledge that he was both. "No, no, of course not. Well, maybe a little surprised. I would not have thought you . . ."

"A fortune hunter?" She chuckled mirthlessly. "Go ahead, call a spade a spade. For I am indeed hunting a fortune." Her brows furrowed as she gazed back at him. "Please, do not look so shocked, Mr. Archibald.

If you knew the level of poverty we have endured the last two years, you would not gainsay me. Believe me, I will do everything in my power to pull us out of financial destitution. I fully intend to secure advantageous matches for one or both of us before we leave Chissingworth. It is our only chance."

Stephen was seeing a new side of Miss Forsythe today, one he was not sure he liked very much. In truth, he understood her desperation. Although he had never given it much thought, he knew that women in general were seldom in control of their own fortunes. In most cases, a woman was entirely dependent upon the men in her life: father, brother, husband, son. As Miss Forsythe had no father or brother, he should understand her need to find a husband. He *should* understand it. The problem was that it represented yet another notion that flew in the face of his illusions of her as artless and innocent as the violets she favored. He just hated to think of her scheming to snare some poor sap for the sake of his fortune. Good God, what would she have done had she known from the start that he was the duke? She probably would have had him in her clutches from that first ignominious encounter. He shuddered to think of it, to think that she was, after all, no different from all the rest.

And he had had such high hopes for her.

She had turned back to her painting. He knew he should either leave or change the subject, but he could not convince himself to do either. Some perverse curiosity urged him on.

"And how is your search progressing?" he asked, bringing to mind the similar question he had asked Miles only two nights before.

She replied without turning around, as though unwilling to look him in the eye. "There are many eligible gentlemen among the party guests," she said. "Unfortunately, my sister has attached herself, for the moment at least, to a most ineligible prospect. Since I cannot rely on her good judgment, I am forced to secure an attachment for myself. It is up to me to marry a fortune."

Stephen's hands, stuffed into the large pockets of his coat, were now balled into fists. But he pushed on. "And have you singled out anyone yet?"

"Not exactly," she replied after a slight hesitation. "But there are several possibilities. Sir Bertram Fanshawe. Lord Knowland. Mr. Brooke. But I am tempted to encourage the Earl of Strickland."

Good Lord. Miles? "Lord Strickland?"

"Yes, he is eminently suitable. After all, he is one of the fifty richest unmarried gentlemen under forty in all of England."

"Fifty richest . . ." By God, it was worse than he had thought. The girl was a professional. "How on earth do you happen to know that?" he asked.

"MacDougal," she replied.

"What?"

She shook her head impatiently, dismissing the question. "I make it my business to know such things," she said. "I have to, if I am to be successful in my quest. Since the invitation to Chissingworth has presented me with this golden opportunity, I intend to make the best of it. I am not looking for just any husband. I am looking for a rich husband. Merely comfortable is not enough. I will not entertain even the remotest possibility of penury. Not again. Not ever again. Lord Strickland is an extremely rich man. And since he has shown more interest in me than in Susannah, I will cultivate his attentions for myself and try to steer my sister toward other prey."

Good Lord, but he felt almost sick to hear such a pronouncement. She sounded so cynical and calculating, not at all the sweet, unaffected girl he had begun to care for. This change in her angered him somehow.

"Well then, if Lord Strickland is such a catch," he

said in a sarcastic tone, "then what about the Duke of Carlisle himself? Is he not also a very rich man, possibly even more so than Lord Strickland? Perhaps one of you should set your sights on his lofty title."

"Oh, no, I could not do that," Miss Forsythe replied, looking the duke straight in the eye. "Naturally, His Grace is also among the fifty richest men. Among the twenty richest, in point of fact. But the man is reputedly not right in the head. There are plenty of other eligible gentlemen of fortune without having to saddle one of us to a half-wit."

Angry as he was, Stephen felt a gurgle of laughter work its way up from his chest. A half-wit, was he? He feigned a cough to cover his laughter.

"Oh, but perhaps I should not speak so of your employer," Miss Forsythe said in a contrite tone as she looked over her shoulder at him. "You must have a superior knowledge of the duke, after all."

"Yes, I—"

"Cath! Cath, where are you?"

The call from beyond the yew hedge reminded Stephen that he must not be seen by the other guests. He often forgot that minor point whenever in the presence of Miss Forsythe. He began to back away.

"Over here, Susannah," Miss Forsythe called. "There's an opening in the hedge just next to the term."

"I will leave you with your sister," Stephen said hurriedly. "If you will excuse me." He darted through an opening in the border just as he saw the edge of a pink skirt coming through the hedge.

Chapter 8

Catherine watched, perplexed, as Mr. Archibald made his swift escape through an almost invisible opening in the hedge. What had set him off so quickly, like a scared rabbit? She would like to have introduced him to Susannah, who had expressed so much admiration for a man who designed gardens.

"Ah, here you are," Susannah exclaimed as she entered the garden. "I wondered where you had got to. However did you find this place? I would never have noticed that opening in the hedge border—and before you scold me, I *do* have on my spectacles. For now."

"Mr. Archibald," Catherine said, "you remember, the head gardener I told you about? He brought me here. Is it not beautiful? It was built around the remains of an earlier manor house. It is kept quite private, he told me, for it includes many experimental plantings. It is not even opened up on public days, for the protection of the plants. The duke, he said, is quite possessive about it."

"It is very nice," Susannah said as she glanced about. "And very kind of Mr. Archibald to allow you to see it. Let us hope the duke does not find out and have your head!"

Catherine laughed. "Mr. Archibald has shown me many special areas of the gardens, for he knows I like to paint the flowers. He brought me here because of the many rare species, and yet here I am painting one of the most common of all flowers."

"Oh my, that is a lovely picture," Susannah said, bending down to examine the painting. "And so very like the real flower. What is it?"

"Clematis. There seem to be dozens of varieties here at Chissingworth, but I am partial to this little purple one. I love the way it climbs up this old wall and gives it new life."

"Yes, it is very pretty," Susannah said. "I am so pleased to see you paint again. How I wish I were as clever and talented as you."

Catherine put down her paintbrush and took her sister's hand. "But you are, my dear. Only look at this beautiful dress I am wearing." She spread her hands out, palms up, indicating the muslin dress she wore. It had been fashioned from one of their mother's old dresses. The jaconet muslin had been in excellent condition. Susannah had raised the waistline, added a fall of lace at the throat, and a French work flounce salvaged from another dress. The effect was very stylish, very *au courant*. "I look just like a fashion plate from *Ackermann's*, thanks to you."

Susannah squeezed her hand. "You are very sweet to say so," she said. "But I really came here to thank *you*."

"Thank me? What on earth for?"

"For singling out Captain Phillips for me," Susannah replied in her breathiest voice.

"Oh, about that—"

"He is *so* wonderful. He is handsome and brave and kind and smart—he is clever, like you, Cath."

"But, Sukey—"

"And he does not stare at me moon-eyed and praise my beauty every five minutes. He actually *talks* to me.

And listens, too, even though I am not at all clever. He treats me like a real person. Most gentlemen treat me like some fragile porcelain doll to be put up on a pedestal and gazed at."

"But, Sukey . . ." Catherine paused, interrupting her own objection as she considered the words of her sister. "Is that true, Sukey? Do most men treat you like a porcelain doll."

Susannah cast her gaze to her feet and twisted her hands together. "Yes," she replied, her voice barely above a whisper.

"You never mentioned it before. Has it always been so?"

"Yes." Susannah lifted her head and gazed intently at Catherine. "But I never truly realized it, you see, until I met Captain Phillips," she continued in typical breathless excitement. "He made me realize that all I ever wanted was to be treated like . . . well, like a woman, not like some precious object."

"Oh, Sukey."

"Captain Phillips is quite the nicest man I have met at Chissingworth. I am so very glad you pointed him out to me."

Catherine was distressed to learn how her sister's incredible beauty affected the way gentlemen behaved toward her. It should come as no surprise that men would behave so thoughtlessly; but it was upsetting to know that Susannah was so much aware of it and so disturbed by it. She was grateful her sister had finally learned that she need not settle for such artificial adoration. Catherine only wished it had been some *other* man to teach Susannah that particular lesson. For it was clear as day that her sister was developing a *tendre* for the terribly ineligible captain.

"He was a hero in Spain, you know," Susannah was saying. "That is where he lost his arm." She suddenly put a hand to her mouth and giggled. "Can you imagine," she said, "that I did not even notice his missing

arm at first? Without my spectacles, he was simply a
blur of green with a lovely, kind voice. But what does
a missing arm matter when he is otherwise so well favored?"

"But, Sukey—"

"I knew *at once* he must be special, for you had
overlooked his disability to single him out."

"But, Sukey—"

"How very open-minded you are, Cath. So many
others would have dismissed him as ineligible simply
because of his missing arm."

"But, Sukey—"

"I just wanted to tell you what a dear sister you are
to me. I am so very fortunate. Thank you, thank you,
thank you!" She bent down to kiss Catherine on the
cheek. "But I must dash. I am meeting the captain in
the rosarium. Enjoy your painting. Good-bye!"

Before Catherine could protest her reservations
about the captain, Susannah had disappeared through
the hedge.

Well, this was a fine mess. Susannah, bless her
naive heart, was lost to the good captain. Catherine
had never seen her so starry-eyed. It was clear she
was halfway in love with the man already. Catherine
knew there would be no possibility of introducing a
rival for her sister's affections. Unless Captain Phillips
was discovered to be a Bonapartist or worse, she
knew that Susannah was well and truly lost.

And the man had no fortune.

Catherine sighed and began to gather up her painting materials. Her heart was no longer in it. Perhaps
she would come back here tomorrow and finish her
picture. But in the meantime she must focus all her
energies on securing a rich husband for herself. If Susannah brought the captain up to scratch, Catherine
and Aunt Hetty would still be stuck in Chelsea without a sou. And so it was going to be up to Catherine
to repair the family fortunes.

As she made her way back to the house, sketchpad and paintbox tucked under an arm, her thoughts drifted to Mr. Archibald and their earlier conversation. It was clear that he did not approve of her mercenary motives. It was strangely disturbing to know she had disappointed him. He had been unable to disguise the contempt in his green eyes, or the scowl that marred his handsome face.

But she had no business thinking of Mr. Archibald's face as handsome, of wishing she could replace that scowl with the lopsided grin that had so charmed her. And no business worrying over his opinion of her. He was only an employee of the estate, after all. He was a nobody. He was nothing. He was not of her own class and so could have no understanding of the situation. His good opinion was not really important. It should not matter at all.

But for some reason she could not explain, it did. It mattered very much.

Catherine puzzled over this conundrum as she neared the house. Her thoughts were interrupted, however, when she saw the solitary figure of the duchess walking along the path just ahead. Her Grace had seemed such a social creature that it was quite unexpected to see her walking alone. Perhaps she simply sought a quiet moment for herself, a brief respite from the hubbub of her guests. In that case, Catherine determined not to interrupt her solitude and slowed her pace.

At that moment, however, the duchess must have heard her, for she stopped and turned around. Upon seeing Catherine, she smiled broadly and waved, waiting for Catherine to catch up with her.

"Ah, Miss Forsythe," she said cheerfully, "I see you have been enjoying the morning sun in the gardens."

"Yes, Your Grace. I often explore the gardens in the mornings, when the light is so crisp and clean. How beautiful Chissingworth is. I cannot tell you how grateful we all are to have been invited."

"You are most welcome, my child," the duchess said. "It is such a vast place, it seems only proper to share it with others. I am pleased you are enjoying your visit. Have you been sketching?" A flick of her hand indicated the sketchpad under Catherine's arm.

"Painting, actually," Catherine replied. "I enjoy painting flowers, and what better place to indulge myself?"

"Indeed. Would you mind very much if I asked to see some of your pictures? I would be very interested to see your work."

"I do not mind at all. In fact, I would be honored to have you take a look at them."

"Well, then." The duchess indicated a nearby stone bench, and both ladies were soon seated side by side.

"Here is what I have been working on this morning," Catherine said, holding out the unfinished picture of a clematis blossom. "I am afraid it is not yet complete—"

"But I can see that it will be beautiful when it is." The duchess took the painting and studied it closely. "My dear child, you are very talented. This is quite extraordinary." She looked up and smiled. "I am particularly fond of clematis, though it is as common here at Chissingworth as any weed. It flourishes everywhere you look. This one, I would venture to guess, is from the Old Hall garden."

"Yes, it is."

"I thought so. How clever of you to have found it. You have captured this special color very nicely. What else have you painted?"

Catherine flipped through the pages of her sketchpad, which was filled with pictures of lilies, dahlias, heliotrope, hypericum, pansies, and violas.

"These are quite good, Miss Forsythe," the duchess

said as she examined the pages. "I am very impressed. Oh, but my son would love these."

"The duke?"

"Yes. He is fond of flowers. More fond of flowers than of people, I am sorry to say. That is why he does not join us." She dismissed the subject of the duke with a fluttery wave of her hand. "But, my dear Miss Forsythe, since you enjoy flowers and gardens so much, perhaps I could arrange a guided tour for you. You could never find it all on your own. I am sure one of the staff would be willing to oblige."

"Oh, but that is not necessary, Your Grace," Catherine said. "I have already imposed upon one of your staff, who has been giving me an expert's tour."

"Indeed? And who is that?"

"Mr. Archibald."

"Mr. Archibald?" The duchess's brow knotted in confusion.

"Yes." Catherine chuckled softly as she brought to mind an image of their first encounter. "He looked at first like an ordinary gardener. But then I realized he spoke so knowledgeably and lovingly of the place that he must be the head gardener. I have been learning a lot from him about some of the more unusual plants and flowers."

"Have you? From our . . . head gardener?"

"Yes. And he always finds the best specimens for me to paint, where the light is just right. It was Mr. Archibald who showed me the Old Hall garden. I am afraid I have imposed upon his good nature far too often."

"His . . . good nature?"

"Oh, yes," Catherine said, suddenly realizing she ought to have spoken with more caution. She had no wish to get Mr. Archibald in trouble for abandoning his duties to spend time with her. "I bumped into him quite by accident, you see. Once I discovered who he was, I began peltering him with questions. I am sure I gave him no opportunity to refuse. He has been very kind. And very generous with his knowledge."

"Has he?" The duchess's eyes narrowed as though pondering a difficult puzzle. "Well," she said at last. "That is most singular. Most singular indeed."

Catherine raised her brows in question, wondering what she had said to cause this odd mood.

"You are very fortunate, my child," Her Grace continued in a more lighthearted tone. "Mr. . . . Archibald . . . has seldom been known to provide guests with a special tour. In fact," she said, tapping a finger absently against her chin, "he is generally most reluctant to allow others into his private world. How very interesting." She turned to Catherine and brightened. "But I encourage you to continue to take advantage of his"—she paused and grinned enigmatically—"his good nature. Oh, and a word of advice. I would not let any of the other guests know of your meetings with Mr. Archibald. They would only insist upon sharing in your good fortune. And, if I know Mr. Archibald"—she grinned again—"he would not appreciate such attentions."

"I am sure you are correct, Your Grace. I have told no one else of him, except Susannah and Aunt Hetty. He implied that I should not." Catherine recalled his swift and undignified retreat when Susannah had appeared earlier. "He even seemed loath to meet my sister this morning. He dashed away before she could join us."

The duchess brought a hand to her mouth as she began to laugh. Catherine had no idea what was so funny, but Her Grace was clearly amused.

"I beg your pardon," the duchess said at last. "It is just that I know how . . . how shy . . . Mr. Archibald can be. I can just imagine him running away from your beautiful sister."

Catherine was thoroughly mystified. The man who seemed so friendly toward her appeared to have a reputation as some kind of strange recluse. Perhaps he really was as loose a screw as his employer, and she just hadn't discovered it yet. Perhaps she should avoid him altogether.

"I suspect I have imposed far too often upon Mr. Archibald," she told the duchess, who was still biting back laughter. "I am sure he is a very busy man and has much more important things to see to."

"Nonsense!" the duchess said. "What could be more important than taking care of one of my favorite guests? I shall see that he is told to give you as much of his time as he can spare. The new conservatory be damned."

Catherine had no idea what that last remark about the conservatory meant, but she did not question the duchess further. The woman was still grinning to herself, and Catherine began to wonder if the entire household was not somewhat addled.

"You must excuse me, my dear," the duchess said. "I had been on my way to meet with Sir Quentin Lacey. But I am pleased we had this chance to chat. It has been most illuminating, I assure you."

"Thank you, Your Grace."

"Oh, and I did so enjoy seeing your pictures. My, but you have a talent, my dear. How lucky you are to be so gifted. I wonder . . ."

"Yes?"

"I wonder if I might be so bold as to commission a painting from you?"

"You would like me to make a painting for you?" Catherine was astonished that the duchess would condescend to so favor her with such a request.

"If it would not be too much trouble," the duchess said. "You see, there is a flower that is a special favorite of mine. I know it is more fashionable to admire the exotics, but I confess I am very partial to roses. Steph—that is, Mr. Archibald has brought in many new varieties from China these last few years.

There is one in particular . . . I wonder if I might persuade you to make a picture of it for me? It is a China rose, called Hume's, or some such unromantic name. It is very pale pink and utterly charming."

"I would be pleased to paint it for you, Your Grace."

"How very kind of you," the duchess said. "There is one spot where this particular rose looks most beautiful. Ask Mr. Archibald to show you the Grotto. It is a bit of a walk, but is quite lovely this time of year. There is a solitary rosebush nestled up against the grotto wall. The Hume's China rose. I believe you will find it worth painting."

"I shall be pleased to do so, Your Grace."

"Good. Good. Then I must be on my way. Good morning to you, Miss Forsythe."

Catherine watched as the duchess turned in the direction of the old conservatory, a jaunty spring in her step. She could have sworn she heard the woman's laughter as she disappeared around a bend in the hedge.

Chapter 9

Stephen took a circuitous route from the Old Hall garden near the western edge of the estate to the construction site of his new conservatory on the eastern edge. He kept to the less frequented paths and skirted the entire southern border in hopes of avoiding any errant party guests.

He chastised himself for so forgetting his need for anonymity. What was wrong with him? He knew the consequences should it be discovered the duke was, in fact, in residence. He had made it very clear to his mother that her guests were not to know of his presence, that he was not to be disturbed. Even the Old Hall garden, regardless of how private, was too close to the house to be safe. What if Miss Forsythe's sister had not been alone? What if she had been accompanied by someone who recognized him?

Miss Forsythe. It was all her fault. His fascination with her had caused him to ignore his usual aversion to Society, to ignore the danger of being discovered. Day after day he wandered the most public of the gardens, courting the disaster of discovery, while hoping to see her just one more time.

He had become obsessed with her, simply because

she did not know his true identity and therefore did not strut and preen in his presence. That, and the fact that she was remarkably pretty. And had big gray eyes sparkling with wit and intelligence. And those intriguing dark eyebrows. And full, pink, kissable lips. And a delightful smattering of freckles across her nose. And because she laughed so easily. And because she showed a genuine interest in his favorite subjects. And because she painted so skillfully. And because she had made a present for him. And . . . and . . . and . . .

She had seemed so perfect.

Until today.

Today that veneer of perfection had begun to crumble. She had revealed herself as a fortune hunter of the worst sort. Oh, he understood her need for financial security well enough. But almost any man could provide her with more than she apparently had now. It was that fierce determination to bag a fortune—a large fortune—that disgusted him. Such heartless calculation was repugnant to him.

Stephen reached a slight rise on the outer edges of the parkland and leaned against a large elm tree. Just below, he had a clear view of the new conservatory. The sight of the sprawling wood-and-glass structure failed to excite him as it usually did. He had no heart for it today. His disappointment and anger upon learning Miss Forsythe's true colors had ruined his day.

Only a few hours ago, when he had first brought her to the Old Hall garden, it had actually crossed his mind that he might reveal to her his true identity. He wanted her to know. Not today, perhaps. But he had wanted her to know. He had wanted honesty between them, so that he could—what?—court her? He did not know. He did not know what he ultimately wanted from her. He had not allowed his thoughts to follow that path just yet. But she intrigued him as no other woman ever had. And he owed her the truth.

But now he could never tell her the truth. He would never be able to know for sure if she was interested in him for his money or for himself. As plain Mr. Archibald, he could be certain. As the duke, he could never know.

And that angered Stephen as nothing else did. He had thought that for once he would be able to know. But now, he never would.

Damn. He kicked hard at the ground and sent a divot bouncing down the slope. *Damn, damn, damn.*

He should have run away from her that very first time. He should have picked himself up, helped her to her feet, and been on his anonymous way. But, no. He had given in to the temptation of a pretty face. He had allowed himself to play out this idiotic charade for the sake of—what? He did not even know anymore.

The only thing he knew for certain was that he was the world's biggest fool.

Ever since he had inherited the dukedom at the age of ten, he had known he could not fully trust anyone. He had learned that lesson very early. He had learned that, in the end, almost everyone wanted something from him. Everyone had an ulterior motive.

He should have remembered that and kept away from Miss Forsythe.

Stephen heaved a weary sigh and pushed himself away from the tree. He might as well go down and check on the progress of the work. Critical ceiling panels were to be installed today. They would be shattering every other pane of glass if he was not on hand to oversee the work. He could not trust the workmen to do it right.

He could not trust anyone.

After dinner, the guests broke up into small groups. Card tables had been brought into the Apollo Salon and several games of whist were in progress. Another group—younger people, mostly—was engaged in a lively game of charades. Yet another gathered around the pianoforte. Others were simply seated about the room in quiet conversation.

Catherine was seated next to the very young Miss Lucy Neville, who was chattering on about bonnets. She went on at great length about the milliner on Bond Street whom she and her sister patronized. After the third detailed description of yet another of the milliner's most fetching concoctions, Catherine's attention wavered.

Her eyes traveled toward Susannah, who was in close conversation with Captain Phillips. Other gentlemen seated nearby vied for her sister's attention, but she gave it to only one man. She had apparently strolled about the gardens that morning with the captain, and during the afternoon outing to the local abbey ruins she stayed at his side almost the entire time. It was becoming more and more clear that Susannah was a lost cause.

Catherine had pulled her aunt aside that afternoon as they had strolled through the remains of the abbey. "Oh, Aunt Hetty. What are we going to do about Sukey? Look at her!"

Susannah had been staring up at the captain with those wide, innocent eyes, a faint smile touching her lips. Her admiration of him was there for all the world to see.

"I suspect, my dear," Aunt Hetty had replied, "that there is nothing to be done. She is lost to him, I think."

"But he is only a steward!"

"Yes, but at least he is gainfully employed," her aunt said. "And I understand the duke is very generous. I am certain the captain will be allowed to maintain his position here for all of his life. There is some security in that, my dear."

"But not exactly the sort I was looking for," Catherine said in a petulant tone. "And she is so very beauti-

ful. Heavens, she could probably have just about anyone with those looks. It is such a waste."

"Oh, but he makes her happy. Have you ever seen
our Sukey so vibrant? I believe she is in love. Let her
be, Catherine."

And so Catherine had accepted the burden of complete responsibility for securing a fortune. She had
turned the full force of her charms upon several of the
other gentlemen. Sir Bertram Fanshawe had shown a
marked interest. He was plain-faced and balding, and
he tended to laugh rather too loudly. But he would
do. Lord Warburton had also been somewhat attentive. He spoke with a pronounced lisp and wore his
shirt points so high that he could not turn his head.
But he would also do. Other possibilities included
Lord Alfred Knowland and the elusive Mr. Phipps.

Her most constant admirer, though, appeared to be
Lord Strickland. He was also the most promising in
terms of fortune. Catherine had determined to encourage his interest almost exclusively. There was not
time to cultivate a circle of admirers and choose
among them. The best plan was to focus on one gentleman, using all her energies to bring him up to
scratch. Since the earl had shown the most marked interest, he became Catherine's prime target.

"Do you not agree, Miss Forsythe?"

Catherine realized her mind had wandered away
from Miss Neville and she had no idea what the girl
had been saying. Something about bonnets, no doubt.

"Naturally, Miss Neville," she replied, hoping she
had not just agreed to anything untoward.

"Excuse me, ladies."

Catherine turned at the familiar voice of Lord
Strickland. "My lord," she said, flashing her most brilliant smile.

"Could I tempt you both with a stroll on the terrace?" he said. "It is a beautiful evening."

"I would love to, my lord," Catherine said, almost too quickly, she realized.

"Miss Neville?"

"I think I will excuse myself, if you do not mind," she said. "The night air does not agree with me, I am afraid. But you go along if you wish, Miss Forsythe. I shall join my sister Caroline in charades."

"Let me send someone for a shawl, Miss Forsythe," the earl said. "I would not wish you to be chilled."

As he turned away, Miss Neville placed a hand on Catherine's arm. "I hope you do not mind me deserting you like that. We can make up some excuse for you before he returns, if you like."

"That will not be necessary. I do not mind strolling with him in the least."

"You are much too good, Miss Forsythe. And he is much too old and too stodgy. I prefer the younger gentlemen myself."

The earl returned with a Norwich shawl and he escorted Catherine to the terrace on the southern front, facing the formal gardens. Others strolled along the balustraded walkway as well as in the lighted garden paths below. It was a beautiful evening, with stars bright and clear in the summer night sky, the scent of box and jasmine, honeysuckle and rose perfuming the air.

It was a very romantic setting, and Catherine determined to let the night weave its spell, if the earl was so inclined.

"What a lovely evening," she said. "Chissingworth is such a beautiful place, is it not?"

"Indeed it is. So, you are enjoying your visit?"

"Oh, I certainly am. And you?"

"Yes," he said after a brief hesitation. "I have always loved it here."

"But?" she prompted.

He turned to her and smiled. "I suppose I am simply missing my daughters. I have never been away from them since . . . well, since their mother died."

"They are quite young, I understand."

"Amy is five and Caro is not quite three."

"And do they have their father wrapped around their little fingers?"

The earl chuckled. "However did you guess?" He went on to tell her of some of their childish exploits, and as she listened, Catherine thought she understood why he would take time away from them to join the duchess's party. He needed a mother for his daughters.

She hoped he was seriously considering her for the position. And she hoped she measured up. She loved children and believed she would be a good mother. And a good wife to the earl. It was a perfect arrangement. She needed a fortune and he needed a mother for his children. Each could provide for the other.

He was a very nice man, if a bit on the dull side. He brightened considerably, though, when he spoke of his daughters. Catherine suspected the quickest way to his heart was through his children, and so she would make a point to show an interest in them. It would not be a deceitful interest, she reasoned, for the benefit of the image of Mr. Archibald's contemptuous green eyes that had intruded, unbidden, upon her thoughts. She did indeed like children.

The earl spoke of the girls' accomplishments, how Caro was already learning her letters and how Amy was quickly becoming a fine horsewoman on her moorland pony. And he spoke of how inseparable the girls were.

"It was the same for Susannah and me when we were younger," Catherine told him. "We were a bit older when we lost our mother—I was ten—but we still clung to one another even so. We still do, in many ways. Amy and Caro are lucky to have each other. A sister is a very special thing. When I was small, I used to think how lonely it would be without my sister."

"Yes, I am grateful they have each other," Lord Strickland said. "I grew up with two brothers and a sister. I used to pity children who had no siblings to play with. I remember when I first met the Duke of Carlisle. We were in school as boys. I used to pity him because he had no brothers or sisters, even though he was a duke. But I never told him so," he added with a grin.

"Ah, Lord Strickland, Miss Forsythe." Lady Gatskyll moved to join them. "Is it not a lovely evening?"

"Indeed," the earl replied. "And did you enjoy the abbey this afternoon, my lady?"

"Immensely," she replied. "What a noble structure it must have once been. But I really came over to have a brief word with Miss Forsythe."

"Of course. Ladies," he said as he swept them a bow and backed away to leave.

Catherine looked daggers at the plump dowager, who was garbed head to toe in brilliant orange that could not have suited her less. Even the ostrich plume that rose almost two feet above her head was dyed orange. The harsh color only served to further inflame Catherine's antagonism for the woman who had interrupted as she had been making great progress with the earl.

"Oh, but you needn't leave, Strickland," Lady Gatskyll said. "I shall only be a moment."

Catherine was relieved, but she had no idea why Lady Gatskyll would wish to speak with her. She had spoken no more than a few words to the older woman during their brief acquaintance here at Chissingworth. She could not imagine what the woman could possibly wish to say to her.

Lady Gatskyll laid a hand on Catherine's arm and leaned close. "I wanted to speak with you, Miss Forsythe," she said in a hoarse whisper, "to let you know that you have not fooled me."

Catherine's stomach seized up into a knot. Oh, no. Not again. What had this woman discovered? What did she know? Whatever it was, she was about to reveal it in the presence of Lord Strickland. Catherine could see all her plans about to be shattered into bits. She bit hard on her lip to keep from crying.

The dowager smiled conspiratorially and patted Catherine's arm. "You may have the others fooled into thinking you have no more consequence than being Sir Benjamin Forsythe's daughters. But I know better."

Catherine clasped the shawl tightly to keep her hands from trembling. What was this woman talking about?

"You see," Lady Gatskyll continued, "I recognized at once the brooch your lovely sister is wearing tonight. You sly things! You must be very close to Lady Lonsdale for her to loan you her jewels. Very close indeed."

Lonsdale! Good heavens, was that not the name of the household from which MacDougal's sister's husband's cousin's wife, or some such relation, had 'borrowed' the jewel case? Catherine closed her eyes and tried not to groan aloud.

"I have seen the marchioness wear that brooch only once or twice," the dowager went on to say. "But I remember it, nonetheless. The filigree work is quite distinctive."

"Y-yes, it is," Catherine stammered. She did not dare look at the earl.

"Do not worry, my dear," Lady Gatskyll said. "Your secret is safe with me. I shall not say a word." She gave Catherine one final pat on the arm. "Not a word," she added with a wink as she turned to go. In the next moment, she had reentered the house through the terrace doors, one tiny orange ostrich tuft floating to the ground in her wake.

At the sound of laughter, Catherine turned to find Lord Strickland smiling broadly.

"Well, Miss Forsythe," he said, "your credit has just risen several notches in the eyes of the *ton* tabbies if they believe you to be connected in some way to Lady Lonsdale."

"Oh."

Catherine was not sure if she should be elated or terrified.

She decided to be relieved instead. Another near miss had been avoided.

But how many more would she have to endure before the month was out?

Chapter 10

He was actually spying on his own home.

It made no sense. It was the height of absurdity. But that was precisely what Stephen was doing. He skulked in the depths of the box hedge near the south front terrace and spied on his mother's party.

He had no idea what had made him do such a damned fool thing. No, that was not true. He knew exactly what had made him do it.

Miss Catherine Forsythe.

She had kicked him in the gut with her matter-of-fact revelations of fortune hunting. She had made him despise her. But instead of just forgetting about her, he had developed this insane notion of watching her 'in her world' to see if she was as cold and callous as she had sounded. Would she shamelessly throw herself at every wealthy gentleman in attendance? Would she flirt and connive and seduce until she got what she wanted? Would she allow liberties and then claim compromise? Was she so single-minded in her purpose?

It was somehow important that he find out.

He could see her even now. She had been on the south terrace for some time. With Miles. The moonlight glinted off her blond hair and he realized he was seeing her for the first time without a bonnet. Had it been only that morning when he had imagined taking off her hat and letting her hair hang free? It was not hanging free, of course, but at least he could see that it was not cropped. It was pulled off her face and pinned at the back of her head in a riot of soft curls. He thought he would still like to see it hanging loose and free. But he had no business thinking any such thing, for he despised her.

His eyes were drawn away from her hair, to her neck, to her throat, and to the expanse of bosom and the shadow of cleavage revealed by the low neckline of her clingy blue dress. He had most often seen her in the mornings, when she was usually buttoned right up to her chin. He had never, of course, failed to note the curves beneath; but as he saw those curves more fully exposed in the flesh, it was enough to stir a man's blood in a highly uncomfortable way. He wondered how Miles was handling it, standing so close as he was.

Though others strolled about on the terrace and the garden just below, she and Miles appeared totally absorbed with one another. More than once, she flashed him one of her brilliant smiles—the same smile that had more than once singed Stephen all the way to his toes. Were Miles' toes burning? He could not tell, but the man was smiling. Dammit, but she had worked her wiles on his best friend; and stolid, upstanding, thoroughly decent Miles appeared to have fallen for it.

Perhaps Stephen should warn him. Perhaps he should tell his friend what he knew about Miss Catherine Forsythe before she got her fortune-hunting claws inextricably into him. Though Miles had been clear that he wanted a wife merely to provide a mother for his children, he deserved better than this. He deserved someone who thought more of him than just that he was among the fifty richest men in England under forty.

But should he tell Miles? Was it really any of his business what either of them did?

He watched as an older woman in a hideous orange dress approached them. As she spoke, a change seemed to come over Catherine. The warmth drained out of her smile in an instant, leaving behind a brittle, frozen mask. Her hands began to clutch at her shawl so tightly that even from his distant vantage, Stephen could see her knuckles were white. What was going on? What had distressed her so? And why was Miles still smiling as though nothing were wrong? Couldn't he see that Catherine was about to faint?

Stephen was almost ready to jump from his hiding place to help her when the lady in orange departed. He watched Catherine's shoulders sag just as the frozen smile slid from her face. But Miles was laughing. Actually laughing. Catherine offered him a weak smile and appeared to compose herself somewhat. But Stephen noticed that her hands seemed to tremble as she pulled the shawl tightly across her chest. Her earlier warmth was replaced by a sort of wariness, but Miles did not appear to notice. He chatted on, smiling, as he led her to a more distant corner of the terrace, out of Stephen's view.

It was not at all clear what Stephen had just witnessed. But it was very clear that something had been said to seriously upset Catherine.

Catherine. When had he stopped thinking of her as Miss Forsythe?

And when had he started caring that she might be distressed, when he had resolutely determined to despise her?

Stephen did not care to examine too closely the answers to these questions. He certainly did not care to untangle the well of emotions that churned within him at the moment. If he once began to analyze the loathing and the admiration, the contempt and the respect, the indifference and the affection, he would surely go mad.

As if he hadn't gone round the bend already, to be skulking in his own shrubbery.

"Your girls seem to be doing quite well for themselves, Hetty."

Hetty took a long sip of tea and sighed contentedly. "It appears so, Isabelle. How can I ever thank you?"

"Tsk," the duchess clucked. "It has been a pleasure. They are lovely girls. Susannah is positively stunning, of course. Catherine, though, reminds me a great deal of your sister-in-law, Eugenia."

"Yes, she does favor her mother, does she not?"

"Lord Strickland seems to have developed quite an attachment for her," the duchess said as she kicked off her slippers and flexed her toes. She stretched out on the chaise and pulled the merino shawl more tightly about her dressing gown.

"Do you think he could be serious?" Hetty asked.

"It is possible," the duchess replied. "It has been almost three years since he lost his wife. It is time he remarried."

"Wouldn't that be grand," Hetty said as she flexed her own toes, propped on the ottoman in front of her. "My little Catherine, a countess."

The duchess silently considered that the girl just may be able to reach even higher, but she kept her tongue between her teeth for the moment.

"And Susannah, I think, has formed an attachment of her own," she said.

"Now that, Isabelle, is more problematic. Catherine, you must know, is not at all pleased with this connection. Captain Phillips does not have the fortune she had hoped to secure for Susannah."

"Perhaps not," the duchess said, "but she could not ask for a better man. Of course, Roger is very dear to me. But he is also as solid and dependable and good-natured as they come. A fortune isn't everything."

"It is to Catherine."

"Then Strickland is perfect for her. He is as rich as Croesus. But, happily, he is solid and dependable as well. I have always been quite fond of him. He has long been a friend of Stephen's, you know, for which he has my eternal gratitude. My son has so few friends." She heaved a weary sigh. "Now, if only Stephen could find a young woman for himself—someone as lovely and sweet as one of your nieces—then I should be happy."

"If the duke keeps so much to himself," Hetty said, "then how can he ever expect to find a wife? Does he plan to place an advertisement and choose her sight unseen?"

The duchess threw her head back against the mountain of pillows and laughed. "That sounds just like something he would do. Unfortunately, I fear he has no plans to marry at all. But, things can always change . . ."

"What made him such a recluse, Isabelle?"

"'Tis a complicated matter," the duchess replied with a shrug of her shoulders. "It all began when his father died. Stephen was only ten, much too young to inherit a dukedom. Imagine being ten years old and suddenly being fussed and fawned over as one of the most important peers in the land. He hated it as a boy and he still hates it." She paused as she recalled the boy Stephen, an almost permanent scowl on his young face as he handled the duties of his title. "I shall never forget the time," she said in a soft voice, almost speaking to herself alone, "when he came to me and said that he knew no one would ever love him. They might love the duke, he said, but they would never love the boy Stephen, for no one would ever let him be just Stephen. I told him that I loved Stephen. But he said"—she paused as her voice choked and her eyes welled up—"he said I only loved him because I had to, because I was his mother. If I had not been his mother, I would love only the duke, just like everyone else. But not Stephen."

"Oh, the poor child," Hetty said. "I never thought what it must be like for someone so young to carry such a burden."

"It was painful to watch him, Hetty, for there was nothing I could do. He was right, you see. He was never allowed to be just Stephen. As a result, he became bitter and solitary and distrustful. He has never had many friends, and as for women . . . if he has had them, he has been discreet about it. There has certainly never been any serious involvement. He is afraid to let anyone get close to him. That is why he keeps so much to himself. He is so seldom seen in public that most of Society would not even recognize him."

Suddenly, Hetty began to chuckle. "My nieces had heard that the duke is kept locked away by his family because he is mad."

The duchess brushed the dampness from her cheeks and burst out laughing. "Mad? Do they really say that? Just like the King, eh? How very droll." She shook her head and continued to chuckle at the notion of her son as mad as King George. "But, my dear," she said at last, "I believe at least one of your nieces has learned that the duke is not mad, though she may not yet realize it."

"What do you mean?"

"Young Catherine tells me she had been imposing upon my head gardener to show her the grounds. A Mr. Archibald."

"Oh, yes," Hetty said. "She mentioned him. The man apparently tripped right over her while she was bending over to examine a flower. Knocked her to the ground."

"Did he?" The duchess found herself laughing

again. "How very like him to be so oblivious of others."

"But what does your head gardener have to do with anything?"

"My dear Hetty, there *is* no head gardener named Archibald."

"What?" Hetty's head snapped around to look directly at the duchess. "No Mr. Archibald? You mean Catherine has been blithely wandering about the grounds with an impostor? And you allowed this to happen?" She fixed the duchess with eyes narrowed in anger.

"Oh, he is an imposter, all right," the duchess said, unable to control the smile that tugged at her lips. "It is Stephen." She watched in amusement as her friend's eyes slowly widened with disbelief. "Yes, it is Stephen, not the head gardener, who has been spending time with your niece."

"The duke?" Hetty said at last, her voice rising in something close to a squeal.

"Yes," the duchess replied, laughing. "His full name is Stephen Archibald Frederick Charles Godfrey Manwaring. Don't you see? 'Stephen Archibald.' There's the head gardener for you. And of course that is precisely what he is, in a manner of speaking. The head gardener."

"And my Catherine has no idea he is the duke," Hetty said, shaking her head in apparent disbelief.

"No, and you must not tell her, Hetty. I believe I know what Stephen is up to. Let him reveal his identity in his own way and in his own time."

"But—"

"You must trust me on this," the duchess interrupted. "I know my son well, you see. Your niece will come to no harm through his masquerade. Quite the opposite, if my guess is correct."

"Oh, but you do not know her. If Catherine finds out the gardener is really the duke . . ."

"But she must not find out just yet, Hetty. This is the first time, that I know of, that Stephen has allowed himself to get even remotely close to a woman. This is an excellent sign, do you not see? He is intrigued enough to allow her to get to know him as Mr. Archibald. As just plain Stephen Archibald."

The duchess watched as her friend's brow slowly unfurled and the significance of the situation struck her with all its force. "Oh!" Hetty exclaimed as understanding lit her eyes. "Oh, my goodness."

"Yes. He wants her to learn to care for him first as the head gardener so that he will know it is not merely because he is the duke!" It was an ingenious plan and the duchess prayed to God it worked. Failure would only draw her son further into himself and further away from life. She did not believe she would be able to bear it. More than anything, she wanted her son to find happiness. She would be willing to bet that Miss Catherine Forsythe was just the person to help him find it.

"We must both encourage her, Hetty," she said. "Your niece could well be the next Duchess of Carlisle. I have never known Stephen to show such an interest."

"Ah, but that could be a problem," Hetty said, her tone downcast. "You see, Catherine will never allow herself to care for a mere gardener. She is hell-bent on marrying a fortune."

"We must trust Stephen, then, to change her mind."

"You don't know Catherine," Hetty said. "She's as stubborn as they come. She has lived on the edge of ruin since her father's death. She will not abandon lightly her quest for a rich husband. She will not give your son more than the time of day if she believes him to be a gardener."

"Unfortunately, Stephen is equally stubborn," the duchess said. "It is unlikely he will reveal his identity until he is certain of her affections."

Hetty shook her head in resignation. "These two stubborn mules could butt heads all summer, Isabelle."

The duchess sighed. "You could be right. Let us watch them closely for a while and see how things progress."

"And if they do not?"

"Then we shall just have to see what we can do to help them along."

Chapter 11

Catherine was inexplicably disappointed the next day when, for the first time, she did not see Mr. Archibald during her morning stroll through the gardens. She did not believe that he ever actually sought her out deliberately, though such a notion would have been oddly gratifying. He would have no reason to do such a thing. It was just that the gardens were his world and he always happened to be about.

But his absence that particular morning was especially deflating, for there had been no posy of violets on her chocolate tray.

She had begun to take for granted the violets would be there each morning, along with the same unsigned note. But there had been none today, for she had disappointed him yesterday.

Catherine did not know what had made her feel she could speak so openly to Mr. Archibald. Perhaps because he was not of her world and there had been no reason to dissemble. His knowledge could do her no harm, since he could never move in the same circles as she. Or perhaps she simply felt comfortable with him because of their shared love of flowers. But as she thought upon it, she realized that their conversations had never been limited to flowers. They usually began that way, but almost always veered off into a myriad of interesting topics.

She had not realized how much she had enjoyed their times together, nor even how much she looked forward to seeing him each day. Until this day when he did not come.

Nor did he come the next day.

She had even gone to the Old Hall garden each morning, hoping she might find him there, tending his exotic plants. But he did not come.

She despaired of ever seeing him again, knowing he felt nothing but disgust for her fortune-hunting ways. But she refused to feel ashamed, for she knew she was doing the right thing. Mr. Archibald simply did not understand the situation.

Besides, Lord Strickland's interest appeared to grow more and more serious. She was almost certain to get an offer from him, in which case neither the opinion nor the presence of the head gardener was of any consequence whatsoever.

On the third day, her morning walk took her toward the French garden. It was laid out as a square enclosure bounded by a high-cut hedge of evergreen oak and bay. A formal parterre was surrounded by trellised arcades twined over by a variety of climbing roses and the ubiquitous clematis. Beneath one of the arches, spires of Canterbury Bells rose in peaks of lavender and pink. A nearby stone bench afforded the perfect vantage from which to paint one of the blooms.

Catherine settled herself on the bench and opened her sketchbook to a blank page. She opened her paintbox, retrieved a palette, and began mixing color for the pink blossoms.

"I applaud your choice of subject, Miss Forsythe, for that is one of the finest specimens in the garden."

Her heart lurched at the sound of the familiar voice

of Mr. Archibald. She looked up at his grim face above her, his eyes hidden in the shade of his wide-brimmed hat. The tight line of his mouth told her he was still displeased with her. She experienced a stab of renewed guilt and shame that she had caused him to be disappointed in her. She so wanted to see that lopsided grin once again. For some reason she could not explain she wanted him to like her. But after thinking she might never see him again, she could not contain her happiness at the sight of him, and she smiled.

Stephen had tried to avoid her. He had not wanted to see her again. He had spent the last few days hovering about the new conservatory, where he knew he had made a nuisance of himself with the workmen. He had stayed away from the public gardens for fear of seeing her again.

But she tugged at his thoughts until he was driven to distraction. Try as he might, he could not force her from his mind. She gnawed at him like a cutworm on flax, until he could no longer stay away. He had to see her again. Just one more time.

It had not been difficult to find her. Her paintings generally kept her in the flower gardens closest to the house. But he had tried five other gardens before running her to ground in the French garden. Stephen was determined to keep his distance this time, to offer little more than a simple greeting, a few polite words, and then be on his way.

But she looked so pretty sitting there, framed by the trellised arch of pink roses, that he had to almost physically steel himself against the simple pleasure of gazing at her. If he was not careful, he would be tempted to stay by her side all morning. But no. He would say only a few polite words and be gone.

And then she smiled at him, and all that well-meaning resolve puddled at his feet.

"But all of Chissingworth is a paradise of fine specimens," she said, dazzling him with her smile. "How fortunate you are, Mr. Archibald, to spend all your days in such a magical place."

"I am pleased you are enjoying your visit," he said, "and that my . . . that is, the duke's gardens have afforded you such pleasure."

He allowed himself a smile and he could not help but think that she relaxed somewhat. Not that she had seemed at all tense. But it was almost as though his smile had melted the last vestiges of her reserve. Intrigued by her reaction, he seated himself beside her on the bench. Now, what the devil made him do such a thing? He was supposed to keep his distance, and yet here he was closer to her than any other time since falling on top of her that first day. Their shoulders brushed momentarily, and she turned sharply to look at him. Their eyes locked, and a sudden shock of awareness trembled in the air between them. She quickly turned away, all at once intent on mixing the pink pigment on her ivory palette. But Stephen had not missed the involuntary tremor that had briefly danced across her shoulders.

So, she must have felt it, too, that ripple of warmth all the way down his arm from the point of their touching. A smile of triumph tugged at the corners of his mouth. She had felt it, too. She was not indifferent to him.

Now, *that* put a new complexion on the matter.

He moved over slightly so that he was not sitting so close. He did not wish to frighten her away. Instead, he began telling her about the various flowers in this garden, and when it had been laid out. They spoke comfortably for some time, that singular charged moment forgotten, or at least ignored.

After a time, Stephen's mulish curiosity got the better of him. "And how does the party progress?" he asked.

She darted a wary glance his way before returning her attention to the Canterbury Bells.

"Any more close calls with Lady Fairchild?" he prompted.

Her musical laughter filled the fragrant air. "As a matter of fact," she said, "there was one incident that almost sent me into an apoplexy." Amidst much laughter, she related to him the story of the Lonsdale jewels and Lady Gatskyll's presumption of a nonexistent connection. Stephen realized she was describing to him the very scene he had witnessed on the south terrace.

"As if that were not enough," she continued, "I have since noticed Lady Gatskyll whispering to other guests as one of us walks by. I am sure she believes Susannah and I are much more than we are."

"And what is that, if I may ask?" Stephen said "You have never mentioned it."

"We are merely the daughters of an insignificant baronet. Oh, we have a drop or two of decent blood. Our maternal grandfather was a viscount. But in the grand scheme of things, we are of very little consequence."

"But, thanks to Lady Gatskyll, your consequence has no doubt increased."

"That may be true," she said, "but it all makes me very uncomfortable. It must eventually be known that I have no connection at all with the marchioness. I have never even laid eyes on the woman. Just to be on the safe side, though, I have decided that neither of us should wear any of the Lonsdale jewels again. It is much too dangerous."

Stephen was charmed and delighted by her animated telling of the story and by her easy laughter. Despite all he knew of her—all the things he preferred not to know about her—he found himself warming to her once again. As she sat there looking so pretty, painting his flowers, and making him laugh, she seemed once more that unspoiled young woman who had so intrigued him.

Until she spoke again.

"My biggest fear," she said, her nose close to the sketchpad as she painted a delicate outline of the flower stalk, "was that I would be unmasked in the presence of Lord Strickland. He had been so attentive, and I could envision all my good planning going up in smoke."

Stephen's earlier wariness fell back into place with the swiftness of a clanging portcullis. The anger and disgust that had been simmering for three days was refueled by her casual words. How could he have allowed himself to be tempted once again by her smile and her laughter and her big gray eyes? She was everything he despised in a woman.

"The earl seems genuinely interested in me," she went on, casting a shy look over her shoulder. "I have high hopes in that direction."

Good God. Was she really going to bring Miles up to scratch? Each night when his friend stopped by Stephen's private office to share a bottle or flask, he could have warned him. He could have steered Miles away from this fortune-hunting cat before she got her claws into him. But Stephen had said nothing.

"It is fortunate that I have drawn the attention of Lord Strickland," she continued in a light tone, apparently oblivious to the change in his attitude. "My sister, you see, has developed an attachment to the totally ineligible Captain Phillips."

Damnation. His cousin Roger, too? Were all his friends fated to fall prey to this wretched family?

"And what, may I ask," he said in his most chilly ducal voice, "makes Captain Phillips ineligible?"

"Just about everything," she said. But then she turned abruptly toward him. "Oh, I beg your pardon. Perhaps he is a friend of yours, since he is the steward here."

"Indeed," he replied, his tone rapier sharp, "he is a good friend."

"Well then, I apologize for speaking so disparagingly of your friend. But you must see that he is not at all what I would have hoped for Susannah."

"No, I do not suppose he is quite up to your standards."

Nor could *he* ever be, as plain Mr. Archibald. She would probably die rather than admit to an attraction for someone so unworthy as an estate gardener. For he knew the attraction was there. He had felt it during that charged look between them earlier, and her shiver when they touched. How hard would she fight it, he wondered.

Out of sheer perversity, he decided to find out.

Stephen rose from his seat on the stone bench. "I am afraid I must go," he said. "There is work at the new conservatory I must oversee. But it has been a pleasure to see you again, Miss Forsythe." He reached down and took her unoccupied hand as he watched her eyes widen with apprehension. "A sincere pleasure," he said as he lightly brushed his lips over her bare fingers.

He turned and left before he could gauge her reaction.

If it was anything like his own, she would need to cool her sizzling fingers in the paint water.

Catherine was not certain whether it was wise to be so far away from the house, alone with Mr. Archibald. She had missed his company for the few days when he had not joined her in the gardens. But in the two days since he had begun seeking her out once again, things had changed between them, somehow.

It had all started with a seemingly innocent brushing of shoulders that had sent an unexpected tremor of pleasure quivering down her spine. And she had been astonished when he had kissed her hand. But he

had dashed away before she could protest such famil-
iarity. It was just as well. Her fingers had tingled so
where his lips had touched them that she had been
unable to resume her painting.

But such feelings were too inappropriate to be considered. He was only the gardener, for heaven's sake.
He was also handsome and interesting and kind, to be
sure. But he was only the gardener. She had no business tingling at his touch. She should avoid him altogether after he had taken such liberties.

But she had not done so. Neither had she protested
yesterday when he had ever so briefly caressed the
edge of her jaw with a knuckle. They had been laughing over something, and it had seemed such a sponta-
neous, almost unconscious gesture that she had not
the heart to chastise him for it. Even so, her skin had
quivered sweetly at the remembrance of his touch.
And thoughts of Mr. Archibald and her strange reaction to him kept her tossing and turning long into the
night.

To be alone with him now, at the farthest end of the
estate grounds, was sheer folly. And it was all her
own fault. She had asked to be taken to the Grotto to
paint the duchess's rose. But she had no idea the
Grotto was in such an isolated part of the estate. She
did not like to consider the propriety of being alone in
such a place with a man. Especially a man who had
such an unnerving effect on her.

Mr. Archibald had been the perfect gentleman during their long trek to the Grotto, never so much as
touching her. The formal gardens had been left behind for some time. The gravel walkways and shrubbery borders had also long disappeared. They walked
now through a heavily wooded area that was almost
magically quiet and serene. Conversation between
them had gradually ceased altogether. Catherine was
lured into peaceful reverie by the sound of the wind

in the tops of the cedar trees, like a gentle tide breaking on the shore.

Suddenly, the copse opened up onto a large pond. Ancient oaks ringed its banks and were reflected in its smooth surface along with broom, willow, larch, silver fir, and a dozen other trees Catherine did not recognize. Long grasses sprinkled with pink and white wildflowers marched toward the banks, and reeds hugged the water's edge, meandering right into the pond itself.

At the opposite end of the pond, a short distance from the bank, stood the Grotto. It appeared to be a natural formation of rocks with a cavelike opening in the front. At the grotto's edge, a single pink rosebush seemed to spring right out of the rock.

"Oh, how lovely," Catherine exclaimed as she drank in the beauty of the sight. Dipper, drakes, and a whole family of teal glided across the water. Two dragonflies skittered along the surface and darted away. "It is like entering a whole new world," she said as her eyes were drawn to the emerald glint of a passing kingfisher. "A bit of unspoiled nature."

She turned at the sound of Mr. Archibald's laughter. "I hate to burst your bubble, Miss Forsythe," he said as he led her along a path toward the grotto, "but nature had nothing to do with it. My . . . that is, the present duke's father had the Grotto built and the pond dug about forty years ago, I believe. The oaks were already here, but the rest of the trees were brought in. He had the bald cypress, just over there, shipped in from Virginia."

"You mean the Grotto is not a natural cave?"

"Not at all," he said as they neared it. "See here? Nothing more than artfully arranged rocks."

"It is incredible!" Catherine said as she studied the ingenious structure. She shook her head slowly and laughed. "I would never have guessed."

"Which was precisely the impression that was intended. Ah, but here is the infamous tea rose."

Catherine bent to study the bush, examining each blossom closely.

"It is called Hume's Blush Tea-Scented China Rose," Mr. Archibald said. "We are fortunate to have them. They came in from China only seven years ago."

"Good heavens, what a fragrance!"

"Yes," he said, "that is one of their many charms. They are quite rare. I am pleased you will be making a picture of one."

"This one, I think," she said at last, indicating a perfect, blush-pink flower, not quite completely opened.

Mr. Archibald placed the painting materials—which he had kindly offered to carry—on the ground and spread out a blanket for Catherine to sit upon. She quickly arranged her materials and began mixing pigments with gum and water. Within minutes she was completely absorbed in her picture. The fast drying gouache required quick work and keen concentration.

"Are you still enjoying the duchess's party?"

Mr. Archibald's question startled her, for a comfortable silence had fallen between them as she painted. "Yes, thank you, I am," she said.

She looked down to see that he had removed his coat and hat and rolled up the sleeves of his shirt. He had stretched himself out beside her, propped up on one elbow as he watched her paint.

How was it that he looked so much more attractive, coatless and disheveled, than most other men did in all their finely tailored elegance? And why did she find his tousled brown hair, curling intriguingly over one eye, so much more appealing than the oiled, artfully arranged locks of other gentlemen of her acquaintance? Her eyes were drawn to his tautly muscled, bare forearms, bronzed from the sun and covered with soft brown hair, and her heart began to flutter strangely in her chest. What would it be like to be held by those strong arms?

Good heavens, what was wrong with her? She wrenched her eyes away from the sight of him and tried to concentrate on her painting. What was she thinking of, to indulge in such wayward fantasies? And about such a man, a man who was little more than a simple gardener. But she was very much aware of his closeness, unnerved by it. She could not seem to dismiss images of his untamed brown hair, his piercing green eyes, those bare arms. Good Lord, was she destined to be one of those well-born women who was attracted to the more earthy, unkempt masculinity of the lower classes? The type who ran away with the head groom? She hoped not. Dear God, she hoped not. She could not afford that sort of distraction just now.

Catherine focused her attention on the rose and silently prayed he would put his jacket back on.

"And does the earl still show a marked interest?"

"He appears to," she replied, wondering why he always seemed so interested in Lord Strickland.

"You are expecting an offer, then?"

"One should never *expect* such a thing, Mr. Archibald. But I am optimistic."

"Does that mean, then, that you can allow your sister's attachment to Captain Phillips to take its course?"

Catherine sighed and sat back to examine the painting. "Yes, I suppose so," she said absently. "If the earl's intentions are indeed serious." She decided some overpainting of the rose petals would be necessary to achieve the proper shading and texture. But first, she must finish the whole. She began mixing greens upon her palette.

"You are fond of him, then?" he continued, distracting her once again with his deep, soft voice. "You would wish to marry him?"

"He is a very kind gentleman," she said. "I would be honored to be his wife." Which was nothing short of the truth. In fact, she would do well to conjure up images of the earl's very pleasant dark eyes rather than those other, troublesome green eyes that she felt boring into her back at this very moment.

"I understand he is a great friend to the Duke of Carlisle."

"That is much to his credit," she said as she began to color in the leaves and stem. "It is typical of his kindness to befriend the poor man."

"I have heard it said," Mr. Archibald continued, "that the earl was very much in love with his late wife."

"I have no doubt he was," she said. Out of the corner of her eye, she noted that he was now sitting upright and moving closer to watch over her shoulder. How was she ever to concentrate? "But it does not signify," she continued, trying to ignore his closeness. "Ours would be a practical arrangement. I would be a mother to his children and he would rescue me from poverty. I do not expect a love match."

"You do not love him, then?" He knelt so close behind her that she could swear she felt his breath tickle her neck. She could not seem to make herself turn around to see how close he was.

"N-no." Her breathing had suddenly become rapid and she was finding it difficult to speak.

"You are certain?" There was no question about it this time. His breath was warm and moist against her ear, causing an involuntary shiver. What was he doing to her? And why did she not simply push him away?

"Y-yes, I am certain," she said at last, unable to manage more than a hoarse whisper. "I do not love him." Her hands began to tremble and she put her paintbrush down.

His hands snaked around her neck and began untying the ribbon of her bonnet. The soft touch of his fingers upon her throat was making it almost impossible to breathe.

"Do you talk with him for hours upon end," he asked, "about flowers and painting and history and all your other favorite subjects? As you do with me?" His low and seductive voice, so close to her ear, mesmerized her into immobility as he slowly and gently removed the bonnet. She stared straight ahead at the unfinished rose.

"No. W-we have n-never discussed those things."

"And do you laugh together?" he whispered as he placed his hands on her shoulders and turned her around to face him. He took her chin in his hand and tilted it up so that she looked straight into his eyes. "As we do?"

His hooded green eyes held her captive. Her throat was too dry to speak. When she did not immediately respond, he raised his brows ever so slightly. "No," she managed at last. "No. H-he is not the fr-frivolous sort."

Without unlocking his gaze from hers, he took her hand and softly, softly rubbed a thumb along her wrist. *Oh, my God.* Her breathing became labored and she caught her trembling lower lip between her teeth.

"And does your pulse race when you are with him," he said, continuing to stroke her wrist, "as it does now?"

No, never, never like this. No one had ever made her feel like this. She shook her head, unable to speak.

He released her wrist and slowly moved his hands up both her arms until they were clutching her shoulders. He pulled her closer, trapping her hands against his chest. "And does he find you the most desirable woman he has ever known?" he asked, bending his head closer and closer. "As I do?"

His lips were unexpectedly soft, and warm from the sun when they touched hers. A different kind of warmth, new and unfamiliar, spread out to every inch of her body in a tumult of new sensations and perceptions. *Oh, my God.* What was happening? She should not be doing this. She should not allow him to do this. But . . .

His lips moved slowly over hers in a way she could never have imagined—tasting, exploring, tantalizing. As his breathing quickened, he grew more insistent. His tongue traced the edge of her mouth and she gave a small sigh of pleasure. He took advantage of her open lips and dipped his tongue inside. The unexpected invasion sent tremors down her spine and all the way to her toes. He pulled her closer as his tongue stroked the inside of her mouth, and she was lost to him.

She had no way of knowing for how long he kissed her, teased her lips, caressed her tongue. All notions of time and good sense had vanished with the first touch of his lips.

At last, he raised his head and her eyes fluttered open. The familiar green eyes that gazed down into hers were dark with desire. His mouth hovered a mere breath above her own. "And do you suppose, Catherine," he whispered against her lips as he stroked the sensitive nape of her neck, "that all the earl's money will make up for the lack of love and desire and passion?"

Mention of the earl brought Catherine back to earth with a thud. She pushed against the impudent man's chest and wrenched out of his arms. "It must," she said as she grabbed her bonnet and rose shakily to her knees. "It must."

She turned and ran from the Grotto, tears of shame and frustration streaming down her cheeks.

My God, what had she done?

Chapter 12

It was perversity, pure and simple, that made Stephen continue to pursue Catherine. He relished this new-found, almost boyish sense of devilment. He was thoroughly enjoying himself.

He resumed the daily posy of violets, but added teasing little unsigned notes encouraging her to follow her heart and not a fortune. He stalked her in the gardens as she painted. Each time she saw him, she gathered up her things and walked away without a word.

She was putting up a valiant fight, but Stephen was determined to win her over. There was no turning back for him, not after that sizzling kiss and her sweet response. Did she even realize that for a brief moment she had melted in his arms? That she had pressed her body against his in a way that almost made him lose control? She would no doubt deny any such response, but he was resolved to break her down, to win her capitulation.

To win her as Mr. Archibald, the ordinary gardener.

Stephen had no idea what he would do with her if he succeeded, for he was still unable to reconcile himself to her selfishness, her greed, her calculated manipulation of his best friend, and her callous dismissal of his cousin as unworthy. Despite all this, he was driven to pursue her, to win her. It was no more than a wrongheaded obsession. He knew it. But there did not seem to be anything he could do about it.

Where once he only sought her out in the mornings when she painted in the gardens, he now pursued her everywhere. Good hostess that his mother was, she generally arranged some entertainments during the afternoons. Whenever it rained, which was seldom this summer, the guests remained indoors. But when it was clear, everyone preferred to be out of doors, and Stephen began to spy on these gatherings. He looked for opportunities to get Catherine alone, but so far he had been unsuccessful. She was either in close company with others—including Miles, damn him— or too much out in the open for him to make an appearance.

But one day, the party gathered for an alfresco luncheon near the Queen's lake. Like the Grotto pond, the lake had been dug and filled, owing nothing to nature. It had been created in honor of a state visit by Queen Anne; hence the name. Grassy knolls bordered the lake and made it a favorite spot for picnics. A boathouse had been added by Stephen's grandfather, and a large number of rowboats were kept tied to the small dock.

The woodlands adjoining the lake, however, had been allowed to grow thick and dense. Stephen kept an eye on the area, as he did with every corner of the estate, and ensured that undergrowth was cleared regularly and paths kept open. Nevertheless, it was a thickly wooded area—perfect for stalking.

He hid behind trees and watched the party dine in relative splendor at the edge of the lake. His mother's idea of an alfresco luncheon included tables, chairs, starched linen, silver, porcelain, crystal, and an army of liveried servants. Not exactly a humble picnic. But so it had always been at Chissingworth. It was expected.

Stephen watched the diners from his hiding place among the trees, reminding himself that he must be careful not to be seen. He located Catherine at once. She was dressed in pale blue with matching blue ribbons on her bonnet. Ash blond curls—curls he now knew to be as soft as they looked—escaped the confines of her hat and framed her face. She was smiling and laughing, and even from a distance Stephen could see those dark, perfectly arched brows quirking with interest.

She was seated at a table with Lord Warburton, an overdressed young fribble who struck dramatic poses as he spoke, as well as Lady Billingsley, a friend of his mother's. A second gentleman at the table had his back to Stephen and he could not discern who it was. He quickly surveyed the other tables and found Miles. He was not with Catherine, then. Good. Stephen also located his cousin Roger, who gazed intently at the blond beauty at his side. The sister, he assumed.

Stephen waited patiently by his tree until the meal was over and the party began to break up. He watched as Catherine strolled along the lake with a middle-aged couple he recognized as Lord and Lady Norcliffe. Stephen darted from tree to tree, following the threesome as they made their way around the lake. Finally, another couple, whom he did not recognize, joined them. The two couples began an animated conversation, and Catherine moved slightly apart from them. He watched in eager anticipation as she moved ever so slowly toward the woodlands. She bent down to admire a patch of wildflowers, and the other two couples drifted in the opposite direction. When he was certain they were out of hearing, Stephen made his move.

"Catherine!" he whispered.

She looked up, saw no one, and furrowed her brow in puzzlement.

"Catherine!"

This time she realized the voice came from the nearby copse of trees. She very hesitantly walked toward them, her eyes darting left and right as she sought the source of the voice.

Stephen moved deeper into the woodlands. "Catherine!" he whispered.

"Who's there?" she said in an apprehensive tone. "Where are you?"

"Catherine!"

She followed his voice, turning left and right as she moved through the trees. When she was far enough away from the lake so that she would not easily be able to run away, Stephen stepped in front of her and grabbed her around the waist.

"You!" she exclaimed, struggling against his arms. "Let go of me, Mr. Archi—"

He silenced her with a kiss.

She pushed him away.

"Call me Stephen," he said with a grin.

"Let go of me, *Stephen*."

"Very well," he said as he dropped his arms. She did not immediately run away, as he had expected, but stood glaring at him, arms akimbo. It was a good sign.

"Why do you persist in tormenting me?" she asked.

"You obsess me."

"So I have noticed. I wish you would leave me alone."

"Am I as unworthy, then, as poor Captain Phillips?" he chided. "At least I have all my parts, if that is what worries you."

The stinging slap was totally unexpected and knocked him back a step.

"How dare you imply that I could be so unfeeling

about the captain's missing arm? What do you take me for?"

"Did you not tell me, more than once, that Phillips was thoroughly unsuitable?" he said as he rubbed at his cheek.

"Not because he has lost an arm! I am not so heartless as that. I am merely disappointed that Susannah has fixed her interest on a man of no fortune. You know that."

"And am I unworthy for the same reason?"

"Please," she said in a plaintive voice. "Do not do this. You know what I want. I have been honest with you about my plans. And I will marry a fortune. I will. So, please, please, just leave me alone."

Stephen stepped forward and pulled her into his arms. "I can't," he said and crushed her mouth beneath his. He kissed her with a savage intensity he had not intended. She struggled briefly. But only briefly. Stephen sensed her capitulation and gentled the kiss. He felt her arms twine around his waist and up his back, and he pulled her closer, tighter against him. She felt so good. So good. His mouth left hers and found her jaw, her throat, her neck, her ears, her eyes, those fabulous eyebrows. "Oh God, Catherine." He could not seem to get enough of her. When his lips found hers again, she moaned softly into his mouth and returned the kiss with equal passion.

When he gentled the kiss once again, she pulled away—somewhat reluctantly, he was sure. She untangled herself from his arms and turned her back on him. He watched the rise and fall of her shoulders and knew that she was breathing as heavily as he was. But she could not face him with her desire.

"Please," she said breathlessly, "do not do this to me. Leave me alone. Just leave me alone." She began to walk away from him. "I never want to see you again," she said as she disappeared among the trees.

Stephen followed, keeping his distance. When she

reached the edge of the copse, she paused and pushed a few stray curls into place. She looked as if she was about to continue on when her back stiffened as though she sensed his presence. She turned and her eyes met his.

"I mean it," she said. "I never want to see you again." She turned, straightened her shoulders, and walked back toward the lake.

Stephen smiled smugly at her retreating back. "Liar," he whispered.

Catherine had only a moment to compose herself before a group of guests saw her, waved, and waited for her to catch up to them. How on earth was she to face them? Good Lord, the Earl of Strickland was part of the group. He smiled at her, but then his eyes darted to the copse. *Oh, no.* Had he seen her there with Stephen? Her hand moved unconsciously to her mouth, as if to hide the evidence that she had been thoroughly kissed. Please, God, do not let the earl suspect. The month was more than half over. She could not afford to lose him now, no matter that her disgraceful behavior made her undeserving of him. Or of any other respectable gentleman, for that matter.

Damn the man for interfering with her life. He would ruin it all for her if she was not careful. For whenever Stephen kissed her, she became so lost to him that the rest of the world seemed to slip away. Nothing else mattered but his lips on hers, his strong arms wrapped around her, and his soft brown hair beneath her questing fingers. It was only when he stopped kissing her that she realized what she was doing, what she was allowing him to do.

And, of course, her allowing it only encouraged the wretched man. He spoke as if he actually had serious intentions, asking if he was unworthy. But how could he possibly think otherwise? She was the granddaughter of a viscount. He was a lowly gardener. Just because her sister had allowed herself to form a horribly ineligible attachment did not mean that Catherine was so lost to good sense. What could he be thinking?

But she knew what he must be thinking, and she despised herself for it. She hated how she responded to him so easily, that with so little effort he was able to make her forget—forget about Lord Strickland and his fortune, forget about Flood Street. Worst of all, he made her forget he was just the gardener. It both frightened and angered her that she should be so susceptible to him. She simply would have to avoid him. That was all there was to it.

She would not let him kiss her again. She would not. She never wanted to see him again.

Good Lord, how could she have allowed this to happen?

If only it had been Lord Strickland who kissed her like that. But he was a gentleman and would never do anything so improper. But she wished he would. She wished he would kiss her senseless and make her forget all about the head gardener.

Catherine took the earl's proffered arm and they strolled with the others along the lake's edge. After a short while, he steered her slightly away so that they walked alone. They conversed on inconsequential subjects for a few moments, and then he began to speak of Epping, his primary estate in Northamptonshire. It was a topic that encouraged Catherine's hopes of an offer. He seemed so eager that Epping should please her—as if just about anything outside of Chelsea would *not* please her. He told her of the estate's history, of the original architecture of Inigo Jones and the more recent renovations by Wyatville, of the size of the stables and the number of tenant farms.

"You will be pleased, I think, to know that Epping boasts some rather fine gardens," he said. "I must confess, though, that they always appear somewhat less impressive after a visit to Chissingworth."

"I do not doubt it," Catherine replied with a smile, "though I am sure the gardens at Epping are very fine. I suspect many of us will leave Chissingworth only to find our own homes suddenly less grand." Especially those of us who return to homes on Flood Street, she thought. "Tell me something of the Epping gardens," she prompted, hoping to keep him on this subject for a while longer.

"Well, let me see. There is a—"

"Excuse me, my lord, Cath."

Catherine turned at the sound of Susannah's breathy voice. Her hand was locked tightly in the crook of Captain Phillips's right arm. "Captain Phillips and I wondered if you and Lord Strickland might like to share a boat with us on the lake. The captain assures me they are quite safe," she said, gazing fondly up into his eyes.

"If Lord Strickland does not object," Catherine said, "I think that sounds quite—Sukey! You are wearing your spectacles!" Catherine was astonished at the realization and unable to quell her reaction. Almost the only claim to vanity that could ever be assigned to her beautiful sister was her aversion to wearing spectacles in public. She had always been very self-conscious about it. And here she was wearing them boldly for all the world to see.

Susannah blushed prettily and nestled closer to the captain. "Roger . . . Captain Phillips, that is, convinced me of all that I have been missing by walking around half blind." She gave the captain a dazzling smile, and he smiled warmly down at her in return. "He made me see that I was allowing my vanity to get in the way of the more important things in life."

"Besides," the captain said, "Susannah is just as beautiful with them as without." He gazed down at her with such love in his eyes that Catherine's heart almost broke at the sight of it. "Nothing as insignificant as spectacles could ever detract from such beauty."

Susannah blushed again, and Catherine thought she had never looked more beautiful, spectacles or no. "And the wonderful thing is," Susannah said, "I can finally see all the beauty of Chissingworth. What a shame it would be to have been here and yet not have seen it."

"You are to be congratulated, Miss Forsythe, on your good sense," Lord Strickland said. "The captain is quite right. There is too much to be missed. Especially while boating on the lake. Shall we?" He indicated that the other couple should lead the way, and all four headed toward the boathouse.

The earl allowed the other two to get ahead a bit. "I have known Phillips for years," he said, his voice lowered so the others would not hear. "He is an excellent man. Solid, dependable, no nonsense. You should have no reservations on your sister's behalf."

Catherine wondered if he realized how much she had objected to their attachment. Was he trying to warn her—as a certain other had done—that she was wrong to insist on a fortune? Well, he need not bother. She could see that Susannah was in love. And though it would have been just as easy to fall in love with a rich man as a poor man, there was nothing to be done about it now.

"And if you do not mind my saying so," the earl continued, "your sister looks positively radiant. I do not mean to imply that she has ever looked less than lovely. She is a very beautiful young woman. But just now, even with the spectacles," he added with a smile, "she is almost glowing."

They both watched in silence as the couple smiled at one another and then laughed together. Catherine thought about the man at her side and wondered if he could possibly ever make her glow like that. But she thought not. There seemed to be only one man who could do that, and he was not to be considered. She looked up at the earl as he watched the happy couple and wondered what he was thinking. Was he asking himself the same question—whether or not Catherine could ever gaze at him the way Susannah gazed at the captain? And would it matter to him if she could not?

The earl turned, caught her eye, and smiled. "Just as a point of fact," he said, "your sister is not the only one smelling of April and May. Phillips looks equally smitten. I believe they must be in love." He looked ahead again toward Susannah and the captain. "I know the look well," he said, a wistful note of sadness in his voice.

And suddenly, a double-edged pang of guilt twisted its way into Catherine's stomach. Not only had she eagerly and brazenly encouraged the earl while allowing herself to enjoy another man's embraces, but she knew she would never be able to offer him the sort of love shared by Susannah and the captain.

But she could not allow such niggling doubts to interfere with her plans. The earl was a widower who understood the realities of life. He had given no indication that he believed she was in love with him. For that matter, he had never hinted that he was in love with her. Theirs would not be a love match. He would not expect it to be.

Then, why did she feel so guilty for not loving him? Why did the look of sadness as he watched Susannah and the captain cut her to the quick?

As the earl handed her down into one of the row-boats, she chastised herself for such maudlin reflection. She must not dwell on such matters or she was doomed to fail in her objective. Financial security was infinitely more important than the absence of love.

Thoughts of returning to Flood Street and certain poverty were enough to renew her resolve to follow through with her plan. And she would.

But no one ever told her it would be this painful.

Chapter 13

"Mind your own business, Mother."

The duchess watched as her son rifled through a stack of scientific journals, taking wicked pleasure in his nervous discomposure. It was a good sign. He tossed a few copies onto the floor and gathered up two or three others that he took back with him to his desk. It was then she saw the painting. Sweet violets, delicately painted in watercolor on parchment. The duchess smiled. Another good sign.

"But, Stephen, I do not like to think of you upsetting one of my guests."

"Who says I have upset her?"

"I happened to be strolling in the woodlands with Sir Quentin Lacey the other day."

"Lacey? Is he your latest cicisbeo, Mother?" he asked, flashing her a lopsided grin.

"Impertinent boy!" she said, dismissing his question with an imperious wave of her hand. "We were having a lovely stroll in the southern wood near the Grotto pond."

"Ha!" He gave her a knowing look. "I have no doubt you were deliberately lurking nearby. Was it not *you* who insisted she must go to the Grotto to paint the damned rose? The same rose that flourishes in the rosarium and a dozen other places near the house?"

"But you must admit, it looks loveliest there against the Grotto wall, in all its solitary beauty." He quirked a brow, and she shot him a quelling look. "The point is, I caught a glimpse of Catherine as she ran through the wood, and she seemed very upset to me. I would swear she was crying."

"Was she?"

"What did you do to her, Stephen?"

"I kissed her."

"Oh, but that is wonderful!" The duchess clasped her hands at her breast and beamed at her son. This was promising, indeed. "You actually kissed her? How marvelous!"

"It was, actually. But she ran away, and you say she was crying. She will not give in to her attraction for me."

"You believe she is attracted to you?"

"Mother," he said, rolling his eyes to the ceiling, "I am not a complete slowtop. I do have some experience with women, you know."

She did not know, in fact. But was glad to hear it.

"But she believes I am only the gardener," he continued in a more sober tone, "and will have nothing to do with me. Told me she never wants to see me again."

The duchess noted the hint of discouragement in his voice, and her heart constricted in her chest. He must not give up yet. Failure could result in his complete withdrawal from the world. She was determined he would not lose this battle. She was determined not to lose her son.

"Perhaps it is time to reveal to her your true identity," she said.

"No," he answered quickly. "Not yet. She would cling to me like a mealy bug on rosemary if she knew

I was the duke. Just as she's doing with Miles. The poor chap doesn't have a chance. She is after a rich husband and will let nothing stand in her way."

The duchess brushed aside a stack of old newspapers and sat down in the chair across from the desk. "Stephen," she said, reaching out to touch his hand, "I think you are being a bit unfair. You have known only wealth and comfort your whole life. You cannot know what it is to want. But those two girls are in a desperate situation. When Hetty told me how they have been forced to live, it almost broke my heart."

"But she told me they were the daughters of a baronet and the granddaughters of a viscount."

"Yes, they are," the duchess said. "But their father was a gamester and a speculator. What he did not lose at the tables he squandered away in foolish investments. His last scheme ruined him completely. He lost everything. Apparently, he . . . he could not face the shame. He shot himself."

"Good Lord. I had no idea."

"And left his two daughters with little more than the clothes on their backs. The creditors swooped down and took everything. Hetty, who had little enough herself, took them in. The three of them have been squeezed into her tiny house in Chelsea these last two years and more. They have sold off nearly every stick of furniture just to make ends meet."

Stephen looked up at her, his brow knotted, a glint of sorrow in his eyes. He seemed about to speak, but only shook his head and said nothing.

"Can you blame her, my dear," the duchess said, "for wanting to protect herself and her family?"

Stephen hunched a shoulder and looked down at the papers on his desk.

"Besides, she is not unlike all the other young girls on the Marriage Mart. Every one of them is seeking a title and fortune, or at least their parents are. How is Catherine so different?"

Stephen's head jerked up and his eyes were dark with an anger his mother did not understand. "Because she is so cold and calculating about it all," he said, his voice tight with contained emotion. "There is no pretense at all. Just pure greed. It is heartless and despicable."

"I think you are wrong," the duchess said in a soft voice, taking her son's hand between both her own and willing him to listen and understand. "It is not greed that motivates her. It is fear. Can you imagine how terrifying it must be for her to contemplate a life of poverty? It is security she seeks, not a fortune. And it is more than financial security she needs, though she may not realize it just yet. Stephen?" she said, looking deep into his eyes. "You care for her, don't you?"

He leaned back in his chair and heaved a great noisy shudder of a sigh. "I'm trying not to," he said at last.

"But you do," she said. "I can see that you do. You can help her, Stephen, to learn what she really needs." Just as she can help you, she thought, if only you will let her.

"How can I help her?" he asked, giving an exasperated wave of his hand. "Besides a fortune, I have no idea what she needs."

The duchess stood and brushed out her skirts. It was time for her son to make his own way through this muddle. There was nothing more she could do. "You will know," she said as she moved toward the office door. "Trust your heart, my son. You will know."

Stephen pondered his mother's words all that evening. It was very distressing to consider the life Catherine had been forced to live. He had had no idea it was as bad as all that. He was sorry she had suffered, sorry that her father had been such a fool. And it would be easy enough for him to resolve all her problems, and his own, by simply revealing himself as the duke. But he would not do so. For reasons too complex to explore, he was committed, now, to maintaining his charade. It was selfish. It was no doubt stupid. But there it was.

Stephen reviewed his mother's words, but was never really sure he understood her meaning. You will know, she had said. Know what? Why must women always talk in riddles? Why could they not be clear and direct, as any man would be?

But then, Catherine had been nothing if not clear. With him, at least, she was plainspoken. He was fairly certain that she was not quite so open with those of her own class. Miles was certainly oblivious to her motives. As the gardener, Stephen posed no threat; he was not worth the effort of equivocation. She wanted a fortune and would let nothing, not even her own desires, stand in the way of obtaining one. Yes, she had been very clear about that.

But there was one other thing—one other thing that was more clear to him than all the rest. And that was the way she felt in his arms, the way she responded to his kisses. She had felt so good. More than good. Intoxicating.

Which must explain why he was once again sneaking around his own estate, spying on his mother's guests.

Though it was early afternoon, they were enjoying a Venetian breakfast on the lawns flanking the Tempietto, a tiny pavilion tucked into a glade in the western stand, and backed up against a heavily wooded copse. It faced a long, rectangular reflecting pool, in the center of which stood an obelisk. Fanning out on either side of the pool were pristine rolled lawns. The Tempietto and its pool, installed by Stephen's grandfather in the last century, had been one of Stephen's favorite childhood haunts. He knew every inch of the tiny temple, including the hidden door in the unadorned rear wall that opened onto a storage closet used by three generations of Chissingworth gardeners to store equipment.

While the party guests dined on the lawns in typical grand style, Stephen prowled the rear copse. The trees butted up so close to the rear of the temple that no one ever came round to the back side, and so Stephen felt relatively safe. He was becoming very good at skulking soundlessly from tree to tree. Watching Catherine, even from a distance, was becoming an end in itself. But he wanted more. He wanted to hold her in his arms again, to steal one more kiss.

When the meal ended and the guests strolled about in all directions, he kept his eyes on Catherine, hoping she would wander closer to the temple so that he could try to gain her attention.

She did. But she was on the arm of Miles, damn his eyes. He could not allow Miles to see him. Or any of the other guests who might recognize him. Stephen held his ground and waited patiently for the right moment.

It came sooner than he expected. Most of the other guests who had come to view the Tempietto began to drift away. Miles had his back to the temple as he spoke to Catherine. Stephen cautiously peaked around the rear wall and waved at her.

Catherine started when she saw him, but composed herself quickly and turned away. Stephen went back into hiding and waited. He watched as she strolled about with Miles, moving further away from the temple, pretending to ignore Stephen. The stiff line of her back, though, told him she was very much aware of his presence. Once, just once, she looked over her shoulder. Stephen waved again, and she turned back toward Miles, chattering and smiling effusively.

He grinned to himself and returned to the rear wall, leaning against it with one foot crossed over the other.

She would come. He knew she would. And he waited.

About a quarter of an hour later, he heard someone coming, and calmly moved to open the door to the storeroom. When she came around the corner at last, he was leaning negligently against the wall.

"What is the matter with you?" she said without preamble. "Are you so determined to embarrass me in public? I told you to leave me alone."

"And I told you," he said as he grabbed one of her hands, "that I cannot." He swung her around, pulled her into the darkness of the storeroom, and gathered her into his arms.

"Let me go," she said, pounding his chest with her fists.

"I've tried, Catherine, but I can't. I can't let go of the thought of you. I can't get you out of my mind."

He bent his head and kissed her. She resisted at first, as he expected. But as he moved his lips over hers softly, tenderly, undemanding, he felt her melt into him. She wanted him. And that only further inflamed his own desire. He deepened the kiss, finally drawing her tongue into his mouth and caressing it with his own.

There was something terribly erotic about the almost pitch darkness of the storeroom. He was aware more than ever of the shape of her, of every curve, of her breasts crushed against his chest. They both seemed affected by the darkness. Their bodies pressed closer together. Hands reaching, exploring, caressing. Their kiss became more lush and urgent.

But Catherine finally pulled away. "Why will you not leave me alone?" she said in a breathless whisper. "Let me go. I never want to see you again. I hate you."

Stephen laughed. "No, you don't," he said and kissed her again.

He felt her instant response, but it was soon warring with resistance. Obviously the woman knows not what she wants, he thought. Is that what his mother meant? Is that what he must teach Catherine, to know what she wanted? And to accept it?

He kissed her deeply, persuading her with his lips and tongue and hands.

But she pushed him roughly away, so hard that he stumbled in the dark against an old lawn roller.

"How can I convince you," she pleaded, "to leave me alone?"

"Not by kissing me like that. You enjoyed it as much as I did."

He heard the sharp intake of her breath. "But that is not the point," she said, her voice still plaintive and tremulous. "You know what I am trying to do here at Chissingworth. And you know that I mean to be successful. Why are you making it so difficult for me?"

"Because there are more important things in life than a fortune."

"Not for me, there aren't." He sensed her backing away, heard her find the door. "You cannot understand, Stephen. You were not brought up as I was. You cannot imagine the humiliation of someone of my class forced to live off the broth of a few onions for the whole of a week because there was no money for food. But I refuse to live like that again, not when I have this one opportunity to change things." She paused, and he heard the sound of her ragged breathing. "I will not allow you or anyone else to stand in my way," she said. "I will do what I have to do."

She walked out the door and into the sunlight. He noticed a glint of moisture on her cheeks and realized how hard she was struggling.

"Once and for all," she said, "I am asking you to leave me alone. Do you understand? I never want to see you again. *Never*." She turned on her heel and stomped away, brushing at her cheeks and straightening her bonnet.

Stephen sagged against the temple wall and wondered why he was wasting his time. She was never going to change her mind. She was never going to give up her dreams of a fortune. Regardless of her own desires, her own passions, she was not to be dissuaded.

His mother was wrong. There was nothing he could teach her. She was a hard-headed, hard-hearted woman. And he wondered why he was wasting his time.

But he knew why.

He had fallen in love with her.

Chapter 14

Catherine flattened herself against the trunk of a large oak, hidden in its shade from any nearby guests. She could not face anyone just yet. Especially Lord Strickland. Her hands trembled, her heart pounded, her face felt flushed, and her lips were no doubt swollen. No, she could not yet face Lord Strickland.

What was she to do? Good Lord, what was she to do? Stephen would not leave her alone. Despite her protests, she knew he would not leave her alone. Was she to endure his advances for the reminder of her stay? And continue to fight her own reaction to him?

But the problem was, she was not fighting it. She was giving in. And giving in. And giving in. And falling under his spell. His deep, rich voice as he whispered her name. The musky, earthy green smell of him. The feeling of his arms around her. And the rest of him. Good God, in the dark of that little room she had felt every inch of him pressed against her. And had wanted more.

No, she was not fighting it. It was too powerful to fight.

Damnation! She was making a worse fool of herself than Susannah. At least the captain was connected to

the duke's family and could legitimately participate
in such gatherings as this. No, this was much worse.
This was unthinkable.

Catherine was falling in love with the gardener.

But, unlike Susannah, she could not acknowledge
her feelings. They did not fit in at all with her plans
for the earl; in fact, they were wreaking havoc with
those plans. If Lord Strickland discovered what she
had been doing only five minutes ago, and with
whom, he would have nothing more to do with her.

But Catherine had no intention of spending the rest
of her life with a gardener. No matter how much fun
he was to be with, or how many interests they shared,
or how attractive he was, or how well he kissed. None
of those things mattered. She was resolved to marry a
fortune, and she would remain steadfast to that goal.

She placed a hand over her breast and felt the calm-
ing of her heartbeat. If only she had a mirror. She sincerely hoped there was no evidence of her encounter
with Stephen. She adjusted her bonnet and fluffed its
ribbon at her neck. She shook out her skirts and
straightened her bodice. She tucked a few stray curls
up under the bonnet's brim. And then she touched
her mouth.

If she closed her eyes, she could still feel his lips
upon hers.

She ran a finger along her lower lip. Was it
swollen? She moistened her lips and prayed they
looked normal. She peeked around the tree to see
who might be nearby before she stepped out of the
copse.

She kept to the edge of the temple, looking up at it
in feigned interest, running her hands along its
carved reliefs. Anyone looking her way would see
nothing more than a young woman interested in the
Tempietto, examining the structure up close. As she
moved toward the front, she noticed Aunt Hetty
seated on the ledge surrounding the reflecting pool,

chatting with Lady Malmsbury. Catherine pretended not to see Sir Bertram Fanshawe beckoning from the other side of the pool. The sight of Aunt Hetty was much more comforting at that moment. She did not care to engage in flirtatious conversation with any gentleman just then. She still felt a bit unsteady, a little too fluttery around the edges, to deal with any of them.

Thankfully, Lord Strickland was at the farthest edge of the lawns, near one of the two marble sphinxes facing the reflecting pool. He was in conversation with Lady Alice Landridge. Catherine was more than likely safe from him for the moment. He was too much of a gentleman to monopolize the attention of any one lady. He had sat at Catherine's table during the Venetian breakfast and had strolled with her briefly afterward. He would not wish to make his interest—assuming there was one—too obvious.

As she made her way to her aunt's side, Catherine watched the earl as he smiled down at Lady Alice. She was such a pretty little thing, with dark hair and big brown eyes. Is it possible he could have a serious interest in her? Her father was the Marquess of Saxe and indecently wealthy. She would be a far better match for him than the insignificant daughter of a disgraced baronet. And Catherine had seen Lady Alice flirting openly with several of the gentlemen. No doubt she, too, had come to Chissingworth in hopes of finding a husband.

The two of them began to laugh and Lady Alice briefly touched the earl's sleeve. A pang of apprehension shot through Catherine's already unsteady stomach. Good Lord, had she been making too many assumptions about his interest in herself?

"Sit down, my dear, before you fall down."

Aunt Hetty patted the ledge beside her, and Catherine sank down upon it. Lady Malmsbury excused herself, saying she wished to have a word with

Sir Quentin Lacey, and left Catherine gratefully alone with her aunt. She could not keep her eyes from darting toward the marble sphinx.

"I would not worry about Lady Alice if I were you," her aunt said.

"Oh dear," Catherine said as she forced her gaze to the clenched hands in her lap. "Am I being so obvious, then?"

"I doubt anyone else noticed, my dear. But I meant what I said. The earl is merely being polite to Lady Alice. I do not for one moment believe he has a serious interest."

"Oh, I do so hope you are right, Aunt. You must know I have pinned all my hopes on him."

"I know you have," Aunt Hetty replied. "And I do not believe you have anything to worry about. You will succeed, my dear. I have no doubt of it."

"I wish I had your confidence, Aunt Hetty. There is only a week remaining of the party. So little time," she said wistfully. "So little time to secure one's future."

"The others are beginning to walk back to the house," her aunt said. "Shall we join them? We can have a nice quiet rest before the evening."

Catherine walked arm-in-arm with her aunt in silent contemplation. She considered her mission to bring the earl up to scratch, but more often her thoughts strayed to Stephen Archibald and their interlude in the storeroom. Why was it so much easier to fall in love with the most inappropriate of men, and yet to feel absolutely nothing for someone as perfect as Lord Strickland?

"Catherine?"

She jerked herself away from her thoughts. "I beg your pardon, Aunt Hetty. Did you say something?"

Her aunt chuckled softly. "Indeed. I have been chattering away these past several minutes. You have not heard a word, have you, my dear?"

"I am sorry. I am afraid I have much on my mind, Aunt. I am not very good company, am I? Would you mind terribly if I wandered off in this direction," she said, pointing toward the north, "away from the crowd? I need some time alone to think over a few things."

"Anything I can help you with, my dear?"

She squeezed her aunt's arm. "Not just yet. I need to sort out a few things first. Perhaps I will explore the stables. I believe they are in this direction."

"You go on, my dear. But do not be too long. You will not wish to be too exhausted to enjoy the evening. I believe the duchess has planned some informal dancing."

"Oh, has she? That should be fun."

"And useful, too, I should think," Aunt Hetty remarked with a sly grin. "Nothing like a bit of dancing to capture a gentleman's attention."

"Then, you can be sure I will not miss such an opportunity," Catherine said, smiling in return. She bid her aunt good-bye and headed off into the woodlands to the north. She made sure that neither the earl nor any other of the gentlemen saw her leave, for one of them would surely insist on accompanying her. And she wanted nothing more than to be alone.

Catherine wandered through the woodlands until they opened up onto a grassy rise from which she could see the formal gardens below. Just to the left, at the base of the rise, was a wood-and-glass building still under construction. This must be the new conservatory she had heard both Stephen and the duchess mention. It looked huge and very fragile, with so much glass. She had never seen anything like it. She wondered what sorts of plants would be kept inside?

" 'Tis an odd-lookin' sort of place, in't it?"

Catherine turned at the sound of the familiar brogue and smiled. "MacDougal! What on earth brings you up here?"

"I be returnin' from the stables, and I just popped round to see how this here thing is progressin'. I come by often just to give it a look. Never saw the like of it. Anyways, I seen ye wanderin' up here all alone. Thought I'd just see how ye was doin' and all."

Catherine was glad to see him. They had all become so dependent upon MacDougal in Chelsea, but she had seen very little of him here at Chissingworth. She welcomed his company. Wandering about alone had not cleared her head at all.

"What do ye make o' this thing, then?" he asked, indicating the huge glass house.

"It is a conservatory," she said, "a sort of greenhouse. I believe the duke and his head gardener are very interested in exotic and rare plants. They can be nurtured in such a place."

"Seems a bit flimsy, if ye was to ask me. Looks as though a stiff wind would blow it clean away."

Catherine laughed. "I doubt that, MacDougal. I suspect the duke and his staff know what they are doing. There is likely a great deal of hidden strength in those thin slats of wood."

"Aye, ye might be right, there," he said. "And is it a good time ye be havin' here, Miss Catherine?"

"Yes, indeed. I am very much enjoying myself."

MacDougal looked at her with eyes narrowed in concern, and Catherine turned away. "Ye sure 'bout that, lass? Ye look a wee bit down in the mouth to me."

"I am just a bit tired, that is all."

"Weel, then." He paused and took a few steps toward the conservatory. "And so, how is young Molly workin' out? Doin' a proper job, is she?"

"She is wonderful, MacDougal. I do not know what we would have done without her. We are all very grateful to you for arranging it."

"Aw, 'twas nothin'. Molly says ye been paintin'. Flowers and such from the gardens."

"Indeed I have. Thanks to you."

"Me?"

Catherine laughed as his dark eyes widened with mock ignorance. "Do not be so coy, MacDougal. I know I owe that wonderful paintbox to you. And what a place to make use of it. Such wonderful flowers everywhere."

MacDougal arched a dark brow. "Aye. Never seen such gardens. Enjoyin' 'em, are ye?"

"Oh, very much. It's almost like paradise here."

"Paradise, eh?" He chuckled softly. "The sort o' place to live in forever, then?"

Catherine's head jerked up and she glared sharply at him. "Have you been speaking with Mr. Archibald?" Stephen no doubt mingled regularly with the staff, including the visiting help. She wondered, briefly, if he and MacDougal were in cahoots, somehow.

"Mr. Archibald?" he asked, a quizzical look on his face.

"You know very well who I mean, MacDougal. The head gardener."

"Ah. The gardener, is he?"

"The head gardener."

"Ah. The head gardener. 'Tis an important position in such a place as this. But, nae," he said, "I dinna know the gentleman. I havena spoken wi' him."

"Oh." Catherine turned and looked out over the grounds.

MacDougal came up behind her. "What is it, lass? Are ye fond o' this Mr. Archibald then?"

"Oh, MacDougal." Catherine buried her face in her hands and gave in to all the wretchedness of her feelings. "I think I am in love with him," she murmured.

"Ah, but that is verra good news, Miss Catherine. Verra good."

Catherine tore her hands away from her face and

glared at him. "No, it is not good. Not good at all. It is horrible."

"How so, lass? Doesna he care for ye, then?"

"Oh, I think he does. But that is not the point. He is a gardener, MacDougal."

"Aye, but the head gardener."

"A gardener, nonetheless. Oh, heavens, I have been so foolish. Can you imagine a more unsuitable attachment?"

He did not respond, and Catherine suddenly wondered why she had so easily confided in him. He seemed so much like family that it was easy to talk to him. But there was no call to burden the loyal retainer with her silly woes. "Well," she said with a shrug, "I shall get over it. I have more important matters to attend to. I am in hopes of an offer from the Earl of Strickland."

"Lord above, ye dinna say so?" MacDougal grinned from ear to ear. "My Miss Catherine, a countess?"

"Too grand for the likes of me?" she said, chuckling. "Is that what you are thinking, MacDougal?"

"Nae, nae," he said, suddenly more sober. "Nothin' is too grand fer my Miss Catherine. I wouldna be surprised if ye was to be a duchess one day."

She laughed at such an absurdity. "Now, *that* would be too grand, I am sure. We shall have to settle for countess."

"Whether 'tis plain Miss Catherine or my lady or yer grace, ye'll always be the same sweet and kind young lass to me. And," he added with a smile, "dinna be worryin' about that gardener fella. I promise ye, everythin' will work out fer the best. Do ye ken? Everythin' will work out."

"I hope you are right." She began to walk down the slope. "I think I will stroll through the gardens on my way back to the house. Are you coming my way, MacDougal?"

"Nae, lass, I think I'll just plant meself here fer a

wee bit and have a cheroot, then be on me way back
to the stables."

Catherine waved good-bye and headed down the
slope. As she neared the conservatory, she spied
Stephen standing near a huge pile of wooden strips.
He was deep in conversation with one of the workmen, pointing this way and that as though giving instructions. She ducked around to the other side of the
structure before he could see her, and then made her
way to the nearby Serpentine Walk, where she disappeared behind its high hedge walls.

She was determined to avoid him. But she felt
somehow more confident, more in control of her emotions after her talk with MacDougal. He had a sort of
comforting presence, much like Aunt Hetty, and
made her feel better about everything. It was strange
how she had come to rely on his wisdom and advice,
as well as his uncanny ability to save the day. She
wondered how a man in his position came to be so
worldly wise.

As she wound her way through the Serpentine
Walk, she reflected upon her initial introduction to
MacDougal. It had been shortly after her father died,
as she discovered the extent of their financial straits.
Hetty, her father's widowed sister, had just offered
her meager hospitality to the Forsythe girls. Though
Catherine loved Hetty, the dear woman was little better off than they were, having been widowed by a
cleric who had given away to the poor nearly every
cent he owned, leaving his wife at the mercy of his
parishioners. A distant relation had left Hetty a small
inheritance, which she had used to lease and furnish
the house in Chelsea. With two additional mouths to
feed, the money could not last long, but Hetty had insisted that their company was more important to her.
They would simply struggle along together, she had
said.

But Hetty did not have much of a head for figures

or economy, and it had been left to Catherine to ensure that what little money they had was used wisely. Just as they had settled in Chelsea, MacDougal had shown up a the door, saying he had heard they were in need of a butler. Catherine had explained to him that they could not afford even a footman, much less a butler, but MacDougal had insisted that he was a very sharp fellow who could help their few pennies stretch even further. The fact is, he had thoroughly charmed all three Chelsea women, with his sparkling dark eyes and musical brogue. Before long, he had settled in as their general servant, a sort of jack-of-all-trades. He even cooked for them on many occasions.

And, true to his word, their pennies had somehow stretched slightly farther than expected. He always had some scheme or other to get something for nothing. Only look how he had furnished them with all they needed for the Chissingworth party. Of course, she did not like to consider for too long the incidents with Lady Fairchild and Lady Gatskyll. She had been avoiding both ladies assiduously.

By the time she reached the house, Catherine had a spring in her step and was ready to face the world with renewed confidence. MacDougal had that effect on her, making anything seem possible.

Her good spirits held through the evening of informal dancing. The carpets in the blue Salon had been rolled up, and Lady Raymond and Lady Norcliffe took turns at the pianoforte. Sir Bertram Fanshawe swung Catherine about with great energy and hearty laughter during a country dance. Lord Warburton had stepped on her toes—no doubt because he could not see the floor over the great cascading folds at his neck, which was immobilized by his ridiculous shirt points. Mr. Septimus Phipps gallantly but soberly led her through a quadrille. And Lord Strickland had waltzed with her.

After their dance, the earl escorted her out onto the

south terrace to enjoy some fresh air. The last time they had stood together on this same terrace, there had been many others strolling about, including, unfortunately, Lady Gatskyll. This time, however, they were quite alone. Catherine's former confidence disappeared completely somewhere in the short distance between the terrace doors and the balustrade overlooking the gardens. She felt inexplicably nervous being alone with Lord Strickland. Her rebellious stomach seized up into knots.

As he often did with her, the earl began to speak of his daughters. He told her of a letter he had received from Amy, telling him, in her childish scrawl, that she missed him. Caro had sent a drawing that looked remotely like a pig but that he supposed was meant to be himself.

"They sound like adorable little girls," Catherine said.

"Indeed they are," he said. "But . . . they need a mother."

Good heavens, this could be it, she thought. He was leading up to a formal offer. She was sure of it.

And all at once, she was reluctant for him to do so.

"They are so young," he was saying. "They need the guidance, and affection, of someone other than a hired retainer. They need a mother."

"But at least they have each other," she said, hoping to steer the conversation away from where she knew it was headed. "Susannah and I survived our mother's death more easily because we had one another to cling to. We have always been close."

And suddenly she was yammering on about happy memories of her childhood, about the joys of having a sister, about surviving comfortably in a motherless home. She even described Dorland and the beauties of Wiltshire. The earl could do no more than nod his head as she rattled on and on.

"Miss Forsythe," he said when she paused to take a breath, "do you think—"

"La, my lord. So much talking has made me parched as the desert sands. Do let us return inside and find some lemonade."

The earl looked slightly taken aback by her declaration, but held out his arm to her. "As you wish, Miss Forsythe."

He led her back to the Blue Salon, where dancing was still in progress. Somehow, Catherine made it through the remainder of the evening. She danced with several other gentlemen before claiming exhaustion and retiring to her bedchamber.

Once there, she fell back upon the bed and stared at the gathered fabric of the canopy above. Why had she not allowed Lord Strickland to make an offer? The offer she had wanted and even expected? The offer she had been so anxious to accept?

He had been about to propose marriage. She was certain of it. If only she had allowed it, even now she could have been betrothed and all her worries over. But some strange, new reluctance had grabbed her by the throat and would not let go. She had not wanted to hear his offer. There was no explaining it; she simply had not wanted to hear it. Perhaps she had been afraid of how she might answer. But that made no sense, for she had been planning her answer for weeks.

She pounded her fists against the counterpane. This was disastrous. She may have just thrown away all she had worked toward. And for what? A pair of flashing green eyes and hands with dirt under the fingernails?

Damn you, Stephen Archibald! I will not let you ruin my life.

Tomorrow she would renew her attentions toward the earl. She would not allow the merest hint of reluctance to stand in her way. And if he so much as hinted at marriage, she would dash off with him to Epping and those little girls so fast his head would spin.

And Stephen Archibald, with his lopsided grin and his smoldering kisses, could go to the devil.

Chapter 15

Everything was ruined, and it was all her own fault. Catherine had spent the entire next day and evening brazenly encouraging the earl's attentions, moving to his side at every opportunity, turning the full force of her charms upon him as often as possible without seeming too forward, and directing conversation toward his home and his children.

But she had received no offer.

Lord Strickland had been all that was polite and friendly, but he had taken no opportunity to be alone with her. He had given her no sign that he wished to renew the discussion he had begun the previous night, about how much his daughters needed a mother. And Catherine had done everything short of openly declaring that such a discussion would now be welcome.

Everything was ruined.

Catherine silently prayed that he would invite her for a stroll on the terrace; but he did not. Even now, the earl stood at the side of Miss Fenton-Sykes and turned the pages of music while she played the pianoforte.

She had lost him. She was certain of it.

Catherine felt the sting of tears building up and knew that in moments her eyes would be brimming. She did not wish to make a spectacle of herself and so quietly stole away from the Apollo Salon and made her own way to the terrace. Other couples strolled about, and so she walked on until she could find a more secluded spot. The moon was high and almost full, and several guests were enjoying the gardens in the moonlight. Catherine walked past them all, spine stiff and jaw clenched as she wandered from garden to garden. She would not give in to her emotions until she was quite alone. She would not disgrace herself in front of other guests.

She finally found the solitude she sought in the French garden. She made her way to the bench near the Canterbury Bells, where she had once sat with Stephen Archibald. But she could not think of him just now.

She sank down onto the bench, propped her elbows upon her knees, and dropped her face into her hands. Tears did not come at once. She felt almost paralyzed with a despair so overwhelming that it seemed she might never be able to lift her head again.

She had been so close, so close to her dream, and yet she may have foolishly thrown it all away. And for what?

She recalled the day after her father had killed himself, when an army of creditors had swooped down upon Dorland like birds of prey. They had taken everything. She and Susannah had been able to salvage no more than one small trunk of belongings, and a few of their mother's things. And most of those items had been sold over the last two years in order to put food on Aunt Hetty's table. There was nothing left. Nothing. Except perhaps for the clothes MacDougal had virtually stolen from the Fairchilds.

How could she return to Flood Street with Aunt Hetty and face that life again? After she had been so close?

But there was still a few days left of the house party. There just might be time to convince the earl that she would welcome his offer. Yes, there was still time. Perhaps it was not too late. But this evening's attempts had led nowhere. The tiny glimmer of hope that all might not yet be lost was almost totally extinguished by doubt and despair. What if he never made an offer, after all?

All at once, Catherine felt a presence at her side. A strong arm wrapped itself around her shoulders.

"Why so sad, Catherine. Have you been missing me?"

Oh, no. That familiar deep voice was almost her undoing. This was all that was needed to complete her despair. The man she could not seem to resist. The unsuitable man who had made her so mindlessly fall in love with him. The wretched man who had caused her to behave in such an idiotic manner with the earl.

It was all his fault. He had ruined everything. She wanted to scratch his eyes out.

But then he turned her toward him and gathered her in his arms.

Stephen knew it was foolhardy to be in one of the public gardens while so many guests strolled about. But, as so often was the case when Miss Catherine Forsythe was involved, he had not been able to stop himself. He had seen Catherine walk down the terrace steps and had followed her from garden to garden, skulking in the hedges so as not to be observed. The French garden was a bit of a distance from the house, and he had hopes that no other guests would wander this far afield in the night.

He had watched Catherine sink dejectedly down upon the bench and wondered what was wrong. She looked so forlorn sitting all alone in the garden. Had Miles at last discovered her scheme and turned his back on her? Had she been denounced by Lady

Fairchild as a fraud? Or, was it possible, was it at all possible, that *he* had something to do with her sadness? Was she feeling torn about her feelings for him?

Such a notion gave Stephen an extraordinary jolt of pleasure. Perhaps he would be able to break her down yet, to win her as Stephen Archibald, estate gardener. It was with this possibility in mind, that all was not lost, that Stephen approached her.

She was soft and warm in his arms, but she had not yet melted against him as she usually did. He rested his chin on her head and held her close, stroking her back with his hands. But something was wrong. She felt like some kind of rag doll, limp and uninvolved, her arms still at her sides. He pulled back slightly and lifted her chin to kiss her. Before he could coax a response out of her, she had come alive and was pushing furiously against his chest. He pulled away, startled at her sudden ferocity.

"How many times do I have to ask you to leave me alone?" she said in a voice that was almost a wail. She launched herself off the bench and stood to face him from a few feet away. Her hands were balled into fists at her sides. "It is all your fault!" she said., "You are ruining everything!"

"What are you talking about?"

"There is an earl—an earl!—who may want to marry me. And yet you keep pushing yourself on me, ruining everything."

"I am not pushing myself, madam," he said, suddenly angry at her outburst. "It has not been necessary. I have not failed to notice that you enjoy it as much as I do. You cannot deny it."

"It is not my fault that you are a skilled seducer, sirrah," she spat, her arms crossed tightly over her chest. "You are loathsome to me. Why can you not see that? You are nothing more than a stupid, ignorant gardener who has got above himself. What makes you think that you have any right to presume upon me?

To seduce me? And you only a gardener, while I am the guest of your employer."

Her voice had risen to something close to a shriek, and Stephen felt as if he had been slapped across the face with a dirty rag. His anger rushed to the surface. How could he have been so thick to believe that she might be different, that she might be willing to love him as a simple gardener and not as the duke? What a bone-headed notion. What a fool he had been!

"I swear to you," she said, "if you so much as touch me one more time I will report you to the duchess. I will see that she has you fired."

Stephen jumped to his feet and almost lurched at her in his rage. "Go ahead. Go ahead and run crying to the duchess," he said, his words rough with anger. "See how much good it does you. I shall simply tell her how easily you melted in my arms." He moved toward her until she was backed up against a trellis. "How you pressed your breasts against my chest, arching against me and almost begging for more." He loomed over her, his face only inches from hers.

"Oh, you hateful beast!" She pushed against his chest so hard that he fell back a step. "You forget your place, Mr. Archibald," she said, spitting out his name like so much bile. "You must have thought it would be some sort of triumph to seduce a woman of my class. But you will not get away with it, do you hear me? You will not get away with it. And if you think for one minute that I am one of those women intrigued by men of the lower classes, then you are more stupid than I thought."

"Oh, no," he said, pacing in front of her, his voice dripping with sarcasm. "No, no, no. I know better than that. Miss Catherine Forsythe is the granddaughter of a viscount and destined for a fortune. She would never dream of admitting an attraction for a mere gardener."

"Well, at least now you seem to understand."

He whirled around at her. "You silly little fool!" He glared down at her and wanted nothing more than to shake her by the shoulders until her head snapped off. "I was only trying to show you that there are more important things in life than money. But, no. You are too thick-headed and stubborn to understand such a thing. Well, I hope you get what you want, Little Miss Fortune Hunter, and live to regret it. And if you think I care even this much," he said, snapping his fingers in front of her nose, "then you are dead wrong. I could never care for such a heartless mercenary. I do not know why I waste my time with you. Go ahead. Run away to your rich lord. He is welcome to you. And I hope he makes your life miserable. Perhaps he will beat you when you dare to indulge in such waspish outbursts as I have seen today." The sharp intake of her breath told him his barbs had reached home. But it gave him no pleasure. "Go ahead. Get out of my garden. I don't want you here. I hope I never lay eyes on your greedy little face again. Do you hear me? I never want to see you again!"

He threw her own oft-repeated words back at her with particular relish. And with perfect truthfulness. He truly never wanted to see her again. He never wanted to be reminded of what a fool he'd made of himself over a girl who was no different from all the rest. Over someone he had once thought was so special, but was not special at all. Over a girl he had once thought he loved.

Bloody hell.

Stephen stormed off in the direction of the old conservatory and his private office. Once there, he proceeded to get very, very drunk.

The duchess enjoyed a clear view of the gardens from her sitting room on the third floor. She watched her son stalk away from the French garden and groaned aloud.

"I think she may have lost him for good this time, Hetty," she said to her friend, who warmed her feet near the coal fire. "He looks furious. Oh, and there goes Catherine in the opposite direction. Good heavens, I believe she is crying."

Hetty gave a loud and gusty sigh. "I suppose she will accept the earl, then, after all."

The duchess turned from the window and joined her friend in a chair near the fire. "Oh, dear," she said. "I had so hoped . . ."

"Do not give up so soon, Isabelle. Nothing is settled yet with the earl. I am sure of it. Catherine would have told me. Besides, you know how these young people are. Things can change overnight. One never knows what will happen next." Hetty leaned back in her chair and brushed a stray auburn curl back up under the edge of her lace cap. She sighed again wearily. "But I confess, I will be very surprised if Catherine does not accept the earl. She is determined on it, you know."

"Oh, Hetty. This is terrible. I believe Stephen is in love with her."

"But so long as she believes he is nothing more than the gardener, she will reject him. A fortune is far more important to her than love."

"Someone should talk to her," the duchess said, throwing her hands up in exasperation. "Explain to her the importance of love in a marriage."

Hetty laughed. "It should not be you, then, Isabelle. You had the good fortune to fall in love with a duke. I, on the other hand, fell in love with a sweet-natured vicar who had not a sou to his name. But I have spoken to the girls often enough about how happy I was with Nathaniel, despite the fact that he gave away every extra shilling to the poor. Unfortunately, Catherine knows too well my circumstances as a widow. No amount of affection will make her accept the possibility of that sort of future."

The duchess considered the matter. Something must be done.

"Perhaps someone her own age would be a better ambassador," she said. "After all, young people seldom believe their elders understand anything at all useful. Especially when it comes to affairs of the heart. Each new generation thinks they have invented love. I know I did."

"Who did you have in mind?" Hetty asked.

"Susannah."

"Susannah? But you know that she is . . . well, she is not exactly the stronger of the two sisters. She is very beautiful, but . . . Oh, for goodness sake, Isabelle. I can hardly imagine Susannah offering any kind of sound advice to anyone. Especially Catherine."

"I think the elder sister may just have the advantage this time," the duchess said.

"Oh?" Hetty quirked a brow and tilted her head toward the duchess, knocking her cap askew. "How so?"

"Susannah, my dear, is in love."

"Ah, yes," Hetty said, a slow smile brightening her face. "I see your point. I shall speak to her right away."

"And I," the duchess said, "shall keep my fingers crossed."

Chapter 16

At the sound of a knock upon the office door, Stephen lifted his head from the desk to see who had the impertinence to disturb him just now, when he was feeling so miserable. The door opened slightly and Miles stuck his head in.

"Mind if I join you?" he asked.

"Oh, perfect." Stephen groaned and dropped his head back on his crossed arms. "You have no doubt come to tell me that I may wish you happy." He rolled an eye toward Miles and saw that his friend had a rather shocked look upon his face. Poor old chap. Probably shouldn't be so sharp with him. Not his fault, after all.

Miles glared at Stephen and then shrugged, no doubt assigning his black mood to the drink. "Not just yet," he said as he cleared off a chair and sat down. "So, your celebration may be a bit premature."

"Celebration, indeed," Stephen said, making a great effort to raise his head and face his friend. "Perhaps you would like to join me, Miles," he said, enunciating each word slowly and deliberately. "I am celebrating the end of foolishness, you see, for I have seen the light."

Miles cocked a brow and a grin tipped his mouth. "What light is that, my friend?" he asked. "I had no idea you were living in darkness."

Stephen shrugged a nonresponse and held out the brandy bottle, offering Miles a drink. Miles took the bottle and the glass Stephen had to be reminded to locate. He poured himself a drink and relaxed back into his chair. "Actually," he said, "I did, in fact, come to tell you that there may soon be cause for celebration. At least I hope so." He smiled rather sheepishly. "That is, if Miss Catherine Forsythe will accept me."

Stephen thought he might actually become ill. It was a moment before he was able to speak. "You plan to offer for her then?" he said at last.

"Yes, I do," Miles replied.

Stephen drew a long breath, then expelled it very slowly. His heart constricted unexpectedly and painfully. He struggled with what to say, knowing he should probably keep his mouth shut. But the drink seemed to loosen his tongue, and he heard is own words spilling out before his brain was even aware of it. "As your friend, Miles, I feel compelled to tell you that the woman is an unscrupulous fortune hunter."

Miles glared at him through narrowed eyes. He took a swallow of brandy and slowly put his glass down on the desk before he spoke. "In what way is she unscrupulous?" he asked.

"In every way," Stephen replied. "In every possible way. I have it on good authority that she came to this party with the express intention that she and her sister find rich husbands. The lovely Susannah has failed her by latching on to my fortuneless cousin. And now Catherine is committed to the project, and she has selected you, Miles, as her prey."

"On what authority," Miles asked, a hint of steel in his voice.

"I have it straight from the horse's mouth, if you

must know. You see, I am acquainted with your Miss Forsythe."

Miles looked astonished. "How so?" he asked.

Stephen was suddenly embarrassed to admit to all that had happened. But he had come this far; he might as well continue. "I met her the first day or so of Mother's party. Literally fell over her in the summer garden. Wasn't looking where I was going, I suppose. She . . . she assumed I was the gardener, and I allowed her to believe that I was. You know how nervous I am about Mother's guests knowing I am in residence."

"She thought you were the gardener?" Miles's mouth twitched up into a smile.

"Well, you know how I look when I'm working."

Miles began to laugh. "But she never guessed who you were?"

Stephen was feeling decidedly flushed with embarrassment. Or maybe it was just the drink. Lord, but this was a humiliating story when it came right down to it. "No, she never guessed. I continued to see her about, and showed her around the gardens several times. There were a few near misses. One or the other of the staff wanting to address me as 'Your Grace' and such things like that. I was such an insufferable bully to them all that she decided I was the *head* gardener."

Miles threw his head back and laughed and laughed.

"Anyway," Stephen said, trying to ignore his friend's amusement, "since she thought I was nothing more than . . ." He paused and recalled the sting of Catherine's words that evening. *You are nothing more than a stupid, ignorant gardener,* she had said. And he rather believed she was right, for he had never felt so stupid in his life. He took a deep breath and continued. "She thought I was nothing more than the gardener," he said, "and so she apparently felt comfortable confiding in me. Told me all about her scheme to snare a rich husband. She had planned it all very carefully. She and her sister need the money, you see. They've had rather a hard time of it."

Miles had stopped laughing and stared up at the ceiling. He swirled his glass in slow circles, the brandy sloshing up near the rim with each turn. "In truth," he said at last, "I do not see anything wrong with her wanting a rich husband. Her motives are little different from my own, after all. Did I not admit to coming to the party for the purpose of finding a wife? It seems to me that Miss Forsythe and I are on the same page. We can each fulfill the other's requirements very nicely."

"But she's so cold and heartless about it," Stephen exclaimed. "She is only using you to achieve some level of security."

"But is that not what most young women are seeking on the Marriage Mart," Miles asked. "Miss Forsythe is no different from the others."

"You have been talking with my mother," Stephen muttered.

"I beg your pardon?"

"Nothing. Go on, Miles."

"Well, in any case, I do not see anything so horrible about Miss Forsythe's motives. Besides, it would not be a completely heartless arrangement. She is really a very sweet girl. I think we will rub along well enough together. With time, we will no doubt develop a certain fondness, an affection for one another."

"But not love?"

Miles sighed and poured another brandy. "You know that I have no hopes of finding love a second time in my life. I do not even seek it. But I need a mother for my daughters, a partner for life. We will learn to care for each other in time."

"No love," Stephen said, shaking his head, "and no passion? Or perhaps you expect passion to come with time as well."

Miles chuckled. "I cannot predict anything in that quarter. I will admit, though, to stealing a brief kiss from Miss Forsythe while we walked near the lake one day. But I fear it was not exactly passionate. It was quite chaste, almost like kissing my sister. I might wish for a little more warmth, but after all, Miss Forsythe is young and inexperienced."

Catherine lacking warmth? Like kissing his sister?

Stephen had to wonder if this was the same Catherine who had melted in his arms on more than one occasion? Who had returned his kisses with a passion equal to his own? Whose kisses were enough to blister a man inside out?

Stephen could have laughed, but suddenly felt ashamed, as if he had betrayed his closest friend. How could Catherine have allowed him to do such a thing? How could she have allowed him to deceive Miles in such a despicable manner? She had no right kissing him like that. How was he expected to resist her when she kissed him like that? And she had the nerve to throw at him that scathing diatribe about supposedly seducing *her*. Bellowing at him like some Billingsgate fishwife when it was all her fault.

Well, Miles was welcome to her, the cold-hearted baggage.

"I wish you every happiness with the . . . the young lady," Stephen said, biting his tongue against the words he wanted to say.

"I remind you that she has not yet accepted me," Miles said.

"Oh, but she will, Miles, you may depend upon it. She will."

"Is it true, then, Cath? You expect an offer from Lord Strickland?"

Catherine strolled arm in arm with Susannah through the Chinese garden. She had asked Catherine to walk with her, and during their walk had admitted that Captain Phillips had made her an offer. Susannah had been positively breathless with the excitement of it all.

"I cannot say for certain, Sukey," Catherine replied. It was the biggest understatement of her life. "I have hopes, but he has made no offer yet."

"But you believe he will?"

"I have been thinking that he might, yes."

"Oh, Cath!" Susannah stopped on the little red painted bridge and pulled her sister into a fierce hug. "How wonderful! I have been so wrapped up in my own happiness I have been blind to what must be a very exciting time for you. I am so sorry, Cath, but even with my spectacles I have been able to see nothing else but Roger." She released Catherine and turned to lean on the bridge rail, gazing distractedly down at the stream below. "But I am so pleased that you have fallen in love as well," she said. "Is it not the most wonderful thing in the world? Have you ever been so happy in all your life?"

"Well, as to that . . ."

"What? What is it, Cath?"

"It is just that, unlike you and the captain, the earl and I are not in love."

Susannah spun around and glared wide-eyed at Catherine. "Not in love? But, how can that be? I thought you wished to marry him?"

"I do."

"But . . ." Susannah looked incredulous and confused. "But, how can you marry him if you do not love him?"

"Have you completely forgotten our purpose for coming to Chissingworth?" Catherine asked, exasperated by all this talk of love. "But of course you have. You forgot it the moment you met the captain. Well, thank goodness at least one of us remembered that we needed to marry a fortune."

"You would marry the earl for his fortune, then? Even though you do not love him?"

"Of course I would. Love is not everything, you know. I am looking out for my future. For *our* future."

Susannah stepped to the other side of the bridge and looked out toward the little slope-roofed pavilion. She did not speak for several minutes, though her furrowed brow spoke volumes. Catherine hoped her sister would drop the subject.

But she did not.

"I do not think it is right, Cath," she said at last. "You should not marry without love. I fear you will regret it. Money is not nearly so important as love. Besides," she said, turning around to face her sister, "a fortune will not bring you happiness."

"But neither will the lack of one," Catherine said. "Good Lord, Sukey, do you really expect me to continue to scrimp and scrape just to put food on the table when I have an opportunity for so much more? Well, I have no intention of living on the edge of poverty for the rest of my life. I will not live forever in the shadow of Papa's failure."

Susannah became very quiet again. Catherine had never seen her sister in so reflective a mood. It was unlike her. "I have been no more content than you," Susannah said, "with the way we have been forced to live. But I think I have learned something very important from Roger."

"And what is that?"

"I have learned that there are different kinds of security in life. There is the sort of security offered by a fortune. But there is also a sort of security born of being loved." She reached out and put an arm around Catherine's shoulder. "I think that is what you are really seeking, Cath. Because that is where Papa failed. He was not a failure so much because he squandered his money. He was a failure because his actions made his family feel unimportant. You cannot deny, can you, that you did not feel he loved you?"

"How could he have?" Catherine replied, her voice choking on old memories, old pain. "If he had loved us, he would have protected us from ruin. He would have left us with some means to survive. But he cared nothing for us."

Susannah squeezed her shoulder and held her tight. "I do not believe that," she said. "I am sure he loved us, which is probably why he put a gun to his head rather than face us with his ruination. But his true failure was in making his own daughter believe she was not loved."

The solitary figure of MacDougal stood hidden among the honeysuckle bushes opposite the Chinese bridge. The morning sun glinted off the silver that sprinkled the dark hair at his temples. His brown eyes were filled with pain as he watched and listened to the two sisters.

He blinked at Susannah's words, and a single tear traced a path down his lined cheek.

"It is the security of love you should be seeking," Susannah said. "Not only the security of a fortune. If you seek only the latter, I fear you will come to regret it."

Catherine felt a pain stab her between the eyes. She did not wish to think of her father and his betrayal. Nor of the love she might have known. It was too late now.

"I do not believe I would regret marrying the earl," Catherine said in an anguished whisper.

"I am sure he is a very nice man," Susannah said. "He seems to be so. I only wish it could be like it is with Roger and me. I wish you could find someone to love instead."

But I have, Catherine thought. Only I have driven him away.

"Dearest Sukey," she said, putting an arm around her sister's waist, "you have given me much to think on, my clever big sister. But I think I should like to be alone for a few minutes, if you do not mind."

Susannah put her arms around Catherine and gave her another hug. "I know you will do the right thing," she said. She gave Catherine a quick kiss on the cheek, turned, and walked down the bridge to the garden entrance.

As Catherine watched her disappear through the trees, she wondered when her myopic, bubble-headed sister had become so wise.

She descended the bridge in the opposite direction and followed the gravel path to the little pavilion. She entered its shade and sat down on the single wood bench.

Catherine wanted to consider Susannah's words. She wanted to consider the security of love. But commitment to that other security, the security of a fortune, still held her conscience firmly in its grip.

When they had first received the duchess's invitation, Catherine knew she would have to grab at this opportunity to find a rich husband. The notion that it was her last chance had entered her head then, and had become lodged there like a fishbone stuck in her throat. She could not get rid of it. Susannah's talk of love nibbled away at it, trying to dislodge it, but the thing held firm. It *was* her last chance.

Besides, there was no reason to dwell on the possibility of love. She had lashed out at the one man she had ever cared for. She had driven him away forever with her hateful words. There was no reason not to marry the earl.

The uncertainties of the night before had evaporated with a few words from Lord Strickland that morning. He had joined her at the breakfast table before leaving with a large group of men for a day of shooting. He had told her he very much hoped to have a chance to speak with her that evening. His meaning, at least to Catherine, was clear. He was going to offer for her after all.

She ought to have been ecstatic. She had already planned a little speech of acceptance. There were only a few more days left of the house party. If she refused him, there would be no other offers. And what would she do? When Susannah married the captain, she would be in no position to help introduce Catherine into Society. The Chissingworth party was her only opportunity. She could not walk away a failure.

And marriage to Lord Strickland would not be so horrible as Susannah thought. He was very kind and considerate and intelligent. His one brief kiss that afternoon by the lake had not set her senses on fire, like those of someone else; but he would make a good husband. She would be content. Not all marriages were love matches, to be sure. Not everyone was as fortunate as Susannah.

But what if her sister was right? Would she live to regret it? Would she always look back and wonder what might have been, if she had followed her heart? Doubt invaded her thoughts with the sharpness of teeth and talons. It tore at her.

What should she do?

Catherine looked up to see MacDougal standing in the entrance to the pavilion, silhouetted against the morning sun. He moved inside, and she saw a look of such concern in his eyes that she almost broke into sobs at the sight of him.

"What shall I do, MacDougal? The earl is probably my last chance."

He paced silently for a few moments and then stopped to look down at her. "He is a good man, the earl, and would treat ye well, I dinna doubt. But ye dinna love him."

"No."

"Ye love another, in fact."

"Yes," she said, choking on a sob.

"Is it fair to the earl, d'ye think, goin' to him wi'out the possibility o' love?"

"I do not know."

"And is it fair to yerself? Ye must think it over, lass, and do what yer heart tells ye. Aye, I think ye must listen to yer heart and not yer head fer once."

But if she listened to her heart, she would throw away everything she had dreamed of. She would miss this one last chance. She had never lived by her emotions—by her heart, MacDougal would say—but had always followed the dictates of sound reasoning and logic.

But there was no logic about the way she felt.

And she did not know what to do.

Chapter 17

She had thought about it all day while the men were out shooting. She had thought about it all through tea and all through dinner. Catherine had considered the situation from every angle and had come to a firm decision.

But here she was alone in the rosarium with the earl and her stomach was a tangle of knots. The moon was near full and very bright and the heady perfume of a thousand roses filled the air. It was a night meant for romance, and just about the most romantic thing a girl could ever dream of was about to happen to her. But she was frightened.

Lord Strickland asked if she would like to sit for a while on one of the stone benches. Catherine's knees had become so wobbly she was grateful to do so. She sat stiffly, every muscle of her body taut with tension, and folded her hands in her lap. The earl sat beside her and reached over to take her hands in his own.

"I think you must have guessed by now why I wanted to speak with you," he said.

Catherine looked at her hands in his and said nothing, trying to pull together her scattered wits. This was the moment she had been waiting for, hoping for.

"I have grown quite fond of you, Miss Forsythe," he said. "I have a great deal of admiration and respect for you. I am hoping you might feel the same for me. I wonder if you would do me the honor of becoming my wife?"

Catherine turned to look at him and opened her mouth to accept. But instead, and without warning, she burst into tears. Great, uncontrollable sobs racked her as she pulled her hands away from the earl's and covered her face. She could not do it. After all her logical consideration, she could not do it. She was consumed with shame and humiliation.

"Good Lord. What is it, Miss Forsythe? Have I offended you?"

Oh God. What must he think of her? She was hateful and he did not deserve such treatment. She took ragged gulps of air and tried to speak.

"N-n-n-no," she sputtered. "It is j-just . . ." She gave a great choking sob before going on. "You are m-much too n-nice a m-man to be s-s-saddled with m-me."

Lord Strickland gently lifted her chin so that she would look at him. Only she could not bear to look at him. "Saddled?" he said in a soft, kind voice. His eyes were so full of concern that she began to feel even more wretched. "You know I would not think any such thing. I would not have asked if I had thought marriage with you would be so disagreeable. Come now, Catherine. Tell me the truth. What is it, really, that has upset you so?"

"I c-cannot m-m-marry you, my l-lord." Her voice was choked with tears and she took a deep breath to try to compose herself. She was making such a mess of things.

"Tell me why," he said.

"B-because it would not be f-fair," she blurted. "I do not love you—"

"Oh but, Catherine—"

"—and I only wanted you for your f-fortune even though I l-loved someone else b-but he is not r-rich and I was in d-desperate need of money and Susannah was supposed to find a r-rich husband but she fell in love with Captain Phillips instead and so it was all up to m-me and you seemed to l-like me and you are very r-rich but Susannah said I should n-not marry you if I did not l-love you and MacDougal said it was not fair to you and he was right because here you are b-being so kind and you deserve someone who could love you but I wanted to m-marry you anyway because of the money and then I got all confused and now I cannot do it because Susannah was right and oh I am s-so s-sorry, my lord."

She paused to take a breath and saw that he was smiling. He reached down and took one of her hands. "I knew about your plan to marry a fortune, you know," he said. "But it did not matter to me. I have not been looking for love, Catherine. I have had one true love in my life and never expected another love match. I never expected you to love me. But I was prepared to offer companionship, respect, and mutual affection."

"Oh," Catherine said, feeling miserably low and wishing he were not being so kind.

"But if you are in love with another, my dear, I would never dream of denying you the opportunity for the sort of happiness I shared with my late wife. I am, of course, disappointed," he added as he gently squeezed her hand. "But your happiness is the most important thing to be considered. I hope that you will pursue this other relationship, even though you say he has no fortune. For there is nothing more wonderful in the world, Catherine, than to share you life with someone you love."

Catherine's tears began again at his words. "B-but we can never share a life together. He hates me!"

"Are you so sure of that? Love can be a rocky course

at times. It is not always easy. But I am sure everything will work out."

Catherine drew a deep breath and let it out with a faint shudder. "I am not so sure, my lord," she said. "I have made him hate me with my obsession over money. I have lost him."

"Do not be so quick to believe that, my dear," the earl said. "If he loves you—and I am sure he does—then you have not lost him."

She looked into his gentle brown eyes and thought for a moment she had made a mistake. Perhaps she did love him, after all. Just a little.

Lord Strickland released her hand and rose from the bench. "Perhaps I should leave you now."

"Th-thank you, my lord, for being s-so understanding. And so k-kind. I am honored that you wished to m-marry me. I am so s-sorry I cannot."

"You have my best wishes for the future, Miss Forsythe. May you find all the happiness you deserve." He took her hand again and kissed it, then turned and walked out of the garden.

Catherine gave in to her tears when he was gone. What had she done? Good Lord, what had she done? And what was going to happen to her now?

Before she could ponder these questions, she heard the sound of others approaching the rosarium. She quickly darted through the hedge gate into the next garden and saw the distinctive row of terms against the high hedge. She realized she was next to the Old Hall garden, a place so private no one would ever find her. She ducked behind one of the terms and came into the beautiful old garden.

She found a bench, sat down, and gave full vent to her despair in a torrent of tears. What was she going to do? What was to become of her? She had thrown away a secure future for the love of a man who could only hate her for the awful things she had said to him the day before. She had rejected the earl, and Stephen

Archibald had rejected her. He hated her. He never wanted to see her again. And so now she had nothing. No one.

What on earth was she going to do? What was to become of her?

The unanswered questions clanged like hammer blows through her head.

Stephen's head still throbbed from the abuse of the night before. It had been years since he had drunk so much. And the irony was that none of it had been able to wipe away his sorrows or make him forget. It had only made him feel worse. He still felt miserable. Only now his head pained him as much as his heart.

He flinched at the sound of a knock on the office door. He knew it would be Miles. And he dreaded what his friend would have to say.

"Come in," he called.

"Hullo, Stephen," Miles said as he entered the office. "You will never guess—"

"Please, Miles, let me first apologize to you for last night, for my abominable behavior. I said some wretched things to you, my friend. I have regretted my loose tongue ever since."

"Do not give it another thought," Miles said as he threw himself rather ungracefully into the chair opposite the desk, which was for once clear of clutter.

"And do you have more definite news tonight," Stephen forced himself to ask. He really had no wish to hear the answer.

"I do, indeed," Miles replied.

The words tore at Stephen's heart like a rusty blade. He had known it would come to this. But now that it had, he did not believe he could bear it. He did not want to hear that his closest friend was marrying the woman he loved. Yes, he loved her. He had stopped arguing with himself over that detail. She exasperated him. She angered him. She provoked him. And most of all, she disappointed him. But he loved her.

"And so?" he managed to say. "Shall I wish you happy?"

Miles smiled and looked so pleased with himself that Stephen was tempted to slap him across the face. "As it happens," Miles said, "the lady refused me."

"Then let me be the first to congrat—What did you say?" Miles's words had just registered, but Stephen knew he must have misunderstood.

"She refused me."

"Refused you?" Stephen tried to quell the tiny flutter of hope that began cavorting in his chest. "But . . . but I don't understand," he said, thoroughly confused. "Why did she refuse you? She was hellbent on marrying a fortune. Why would she pass up the opportunity to be a rich countess?"

This did not make any sense. She had been so definite about it. She wanted a rich husband and it was going to be Miles. She had made herself perfectly clear on that point. And so what had happened? "Good God!" he blurted. "Have others been courting her as well? Does she have other prospects? Damnation, Miles, did she toss you over for someone else?"

"None of the other guests is courting her, I assure you," he replied. What was that damned sparkle in Miles's eyes? Why did he seem so pleased to be rejected?

"None of this is making sense," he said. "Why did she refuse you, then? And for God's sake, why are you so bloody cheerful about it?"

Miles chuckled, and Stephen was once again tempted to strike him. If he did not get on with the story, Stephen swore to himself that he would do so. "It appears Miss Forsythe cannot marry me because she is in love with . . . with someone else."

Stephen's breath constricted as though he had been

punched in the stomach. "Someone else?" he muttered.

Miles laughed and reached across to desk to clap Stephen on the shoulder. "Well, what are you waiting for?" he said, smiling broadly. "You have finally found a woman who loves you for yourself and not your title. She still believes you are a gardener with no money, you know."

Stephen stared openmouthed at Miles. His words threw Stephen's heart into a wild disorder.

She loved him?

"She also believes," Miles continued, "that you hate her. Do you?"

"Good God, no! No, I . . ." Stephen stopped. Was he really about to admit that he was in love with the woman his friend had wanted to marry? And had been for most of the time Miles had courted her? What a wretch he was. What would Miles think of him?

But she loved him. Miles said she loved him.

"I'm sorry, Miles. Truly I am. I never meant for it to happen."

"You do love her, then?"

"Yes. Yes, God help me, I do."

"Then you have nothing to apologize for," Miles said. "It was worth anything just to hear you say that." Miles began to laugh again, and Stephen felt so light-headed that he laughed along with him.

"I must say," Miles continued, "my vanity was bruised a bit at first. I had been so sure of myself, you see. But you had said nothing, you dog, or I might have saved myself from an embarrassing disappointment. But it is all eclipsed by the prospect of seeing you happy at last."

"You are sure it is me she is in love with?" Stephen asked, suddenly nervous and uncertain. "Did she actually mention me by name?"

"Good God, Stephen! Don't be such a sapskull. Are

you going to let her walk out of your life while you sit there and think about it?"

"No! No, I am not." He rose so quickly that the chair was knocked out from under him and clattered to the floor. He reached the door before he realized he did not know where he was going. He had no idea where she was. What if she was in the house, gathered somewhere with all the other guests? He could not simply make an appearance in one of the drawing rooms after a month in hiding. He turned an imploring look on his friend. "Miles, where—"

"I left her in the rosarium," he said.

"Thanks, old chap." Stephen turned to rush out the door, but stopped and came back in. He held his hand out and Miles clasped it. "Thank you."

Miles smiled and nodded, and then Stephen was off, leaving his friend sitting alone in his office. He hurried through the old conservatory and out its door, keeping close to the brick walls. It was a bright evening, and still somewhat early. Other guests were sure to be about.

He crept along the hedge borders as he made his way toward the rosarium. He spied several strolling couples, but dashed away before they could see him. When he reached the rosarium, he went crashing inside in his impatience to see her. Five or six startled guests turned to look at him and he ducked immediately back out. *Damnation.* But Catherine was not among them. Where had she gone? What if she had returned to the house? He could not follow her there.

The strong smell of cheroot caused Stephen to turn around. A tall, dark man was leaning against an arbor in the walkway between the rosarium and the summer garden. His face was hidden in the shadows, but Stephen could see the glow of his lit cheroot.

"Yer Grace," he man said, doffing his cap.

Stephen nodded a distracted acknowledgment and

continued to wonder where he should look next to find Catherine.

"Ye'll find Miss Catherine in the Old Hall garden," the man said, his voice tinged with a slight burr.

Of course! He should have known she'd be there. He rushed down the path without a word, but stopped suddenly. Who was that fellow? He did not have any Scotsmen on the staff, as far as he knew. And yet he had recognized Stephen as the duke. He turned back toward the arbor, but the man was gone. The smell of cheroot still hung in the air.

Who the devil had it been?

Stephen shrugged and hurried down the gravel path. It did not matter. There was only one thing on his mind at the moment.

He must find Catherine.

Chapter 18

Catherine sat cradled in Stephen's arms. He held her so tightly she thought he never meant to let go. And that was just fine with her. She knew now that this was where she belonged.

"I am so s-sorry," she stammered, burrowing her head against his shoulder. She had wept buckets of tears this night and could not seem to stop. "I did not really mean any of those horrible things I said to you before. I was so hateful to you."

"Hush, love. It doesn't matter."

"But you do not understand. I know you must have thought I was heartless and greedy. But I was so scared. I thought it was my last chance. I didn't want to lose everything like my father did."

"Hush, love."

"But I really believed I needed a fortune, you see. I really believed I could not be happy without one. But I know now I was wrong. And after I said all those hateful things to you!"

"Shh. It doesn't matter."

"But I didn't mean it, Stephen! I didn't mean it. You are not an ignorant gardener. How could I ever have said such a thing? You are the most wonderful man in the whole world. And you are not at all ignorant. You know so many things about plants and history and you've been to America and you've taught me so much and you are such fun to be with and you make me laugh and you find me flowers to paint and you look so handsome that you make me weak in the knees and you make me feel tingly all over when you kiss me. Oh, how I wish I had never said those horrid things to you! Can you ever forgive me?"

"It doesn't matter, love. None of that matters anymore." He lifted her chin and kissed her so tenderly she thought her heart would break from the sweetness of it.

He pulled back and looked into her eyes. "I love you, Catherine," he said, and then pulled her close against him once more.

Her heart soared at his words. How could she ever have believed it was not important? She winced at the thought of how close she had come to never knowing the joy of hearing those words.

"When I heard you had refused the earl . . ." He seemed unable to continue. His voice was choked with emotion. Catherine wondered briefly how he had known about her refusal, but did not really care. "When I heard that," he continued at last, "I was afraid to hope it might be because you loved me. Do you, sweet Catherine?"

She lifted her head from his shoulder and looked deeply into his eyes. "I do," she said. "I do love you."

"Oh, God, Catherine." His lips captured hers in a kiss so lush, so full of promise, she thought she might drown in the hot, sweet taste of him.

After a long interval during which they were lost to one another, Stephen lifted his head and smiled. He took her face ever so gently in his hands. "Will you marry me?"

Her heart began to flutter in her breast, like the wing beats of a thousand butterflies. This was what she wanted. She had been foolish to think otherwise. After denying them for so long, she was unexpectedly shaken by the force of her feelings for him. How could she have ever doubted? She choked back a lump in her throat. "Oh, Stephen," was all she could seem to say.

Uncertainty gathered in his green eyes and she realized he still believed she still might reject him for a fortune. How could she be so cruel to allow him to think so?

"Stephen, I—"

"You love it here at Chissingworth, do you not?" he interrupted. "You love the flowers and the gardens?"

"Of course I do. It is the nearest thing to paradise on earth."

"Then, come live with me here, Catherine. Come live with me in this garden paradise, and we shall be forever happy together."

"I would love nothing more," she said and kissed him.

"Then, you will marry me? You will live here at Chissingworth with me?"

"I would be honored to marry you, Stephen."

He crushed her to him so tightly she thought her bones might break. But it did not matter. It felt so good, so safe, to be in his arms. He rocked her gently back and forth as he held her, whispering words of love in her ear. She never wanted to leave this spot. She wanted to stay here in his arms forever.

And she could. For she was going to marry Stephen and live with him at Chissingworth.

But a niggling curiosity, a twinge of the old concern tugged at her. She had to understand. It did not really matter. It was purely a matter of curiosity, for they had never spoken of it. She merely wanted to know.

She lifted her head from his shoulder and looked at him. "Where . . . where exactly would we live,

Stephen? Do you . . . do you have a cottage on the estate?"

Catherine saw a flicker of concern in his eyes and regretted her words instantly.

"Would that be so terrible?" he asked. The uncertainty in his voice tore at her heart.

She flung her arms around his neck and hugged him tightly. "No, of course not," she whispered. "I would be happy living anywhere with you. Deliriously happy. Even a one-room cottage would be sufficient, so long as we are together."

He began to chuckle and she felt him relax. "Well, it is not quite so bad as that," he said, a hint of amusement in his voice. "But do you really mean it? You would marry me, with no fortune and no prospects?"

"Of course I mean it," she said while feathering kisses over his face. "I love you, Stephen." She stopped kissing him and looked directly into his eyes. "You must try to forgive me for being so very foolish. But I have learned my lesson. Susannah would be very proud of me. For I have learned that love is worth all the fortunes of the world."

Stephen's heart was so full to bursting he wondered that it did not explode right out of his chest. She really loved him. She really wished to marry him.

And she still had no idea that he was the duke.

He could not say for certain if this was the end he had hoped for from the beginning, from those first days of his masquerade. But somewhere along the line, he knew it had become so. It had become his unswerving objective that he could make a woman fall in love with him for himself and not as the duke. But not just any woman. This woman. Catherine. He had wanted her all along, but he had also hoped that she would want him.

And she did. Stephen could never have predicted the intensity of emotion such a declaration would have on him. He was almost overcome by it. All he wanted was to hold her and hold her and never let go.

He could still hardly believe it. She loved him. She really loved him. Oh, she was a bit nervous about living in a one-room shack, but she was willing to do so. What would she do when she learned that the grand house at Chissingworth was to be her home instead?

Out of sheer mischief, Stephen decided not to tell her just yet. A wicked plan had begun to take shape in his mind. He bit back a smile as he considered he may just have the perfect way to get back at her for calling him a stupid gardener. It was low. It was shameless. But he could not resist.

He pulled Catherine onto his lap and tucked her head beneath his chin. She nestled closer and he felt a swelling of such love for her he wondered that he could even consider pulling such a rig. She would probably kill him. But it was too deliciously irresistible.

"I have heard," he said, "that tomorrow night is the duchess's grand ball."

"Yes," she said wistfully as she absently played with the buttons on his waistcoat. "It is the culmination of the house party."

"I suppose you have a fine new gown for the occasion?"

"Well, it is not new, of course. Merely another of the Fairchild dresses altered by Susannah. But it is quite pretty, I think."

"What color is it?"

"Pink. Why?"

"Just curious. Have you heard that His Grace might put in an appearance?"

"The duke?"

"Yes. You have not heard that rumor?"

"No," she said, her voice full of surprise. She had stopped toying with his buttons. "I had not heard.

How very curious. I did not think he ever appeared at his mother's parties."

Stephen was grinning roguishly above her head. He could not help himself. "The buzz among the staff is that he is coming to the ball to announce his betrothal."

"Really? The duke is to marry? How fascinating."

It was all Stephen could do not to begin snickering. He could just imagine what Catherine was thinking. The poor old dim-witted duke was to take a bride. Who on earth would have such a pitiful creature?

"Who is he to marry?" she asked, and Stephen had to bite the inside of his cheek to keep from laughing.

"I do not know. But I imagine you will find out at the ball when the announcement is made."

She turned in his arms and put her hands on his shoulders. "How I wish you could come with me to the ball, Stephen. I would love to dance with you."

He shook his head and brushed a kiss against her lips.

"I understand, my love," she said. "I know you cannot attend the ball. But it will be no fun for me without you there. I wish I did not have to go."

"Oh, but you must," he said. "The duchess would be offended."

"I know she would. And she has been so kind and hospitable. I must make at least a brief appearance out of respect."

"You must be there for the duke's announcement."

"Must I?"

"It is the proper thing to do, my love."

"Yes, of course." She breathed a sigh. "But I shall sneak away directly afterward and meet you here."

Stephen lifted her off his lap, pulled her to her feet, and took her in his arms. "Tomorrow, then," he said, "we shall dance together under the stars and celebrate our own betrothal."

* * *

"Oh but, Stephen! That is wonderful!"

The duchess threw her arms around her son's neck and hugged him close. "It is, isn't it," he said. She whooped with surprise when he lifted her by the waist and swung her around and around. When he finally settled her back to earth, she laid her hands against his chest to regain her balance. He looked down at her and a huge grin split his face from ear to ear.

His smile brought a lump to her throat. She had never seen him this happy. Not since he was a carefree little boy, before he became the duke. She had hoped and hoped that this would happen, that he would finally find a woman who loved him for himself alone. She had believed Catherine Forsythe just might be the one. But that business about a fortune and Lord Strickland's interest had been powerful concerns. She was happier than she could say that Catherine had shown the fortitude to follow her heart and not her empty purse.

But he had not yet revealed to her his true identity. Now that he had the proof of her love, she wondered what stopped him.

"And she has no idea you are Carlisle?" she asked.

"None," he replied with a devilish grin.

"And when, may I ask, do you think you might tell her? Do you plan to wait until after the ceremony? Or until after your wedding night? Or perhaps until after your first child is born?"

Stephen laughed. She did not know when she had seen him laugh so much. "Not quite that long," he said. "Only until the announcement. And that is where I need your help, Mother."

The duchess stood slack-jawed with astonishment as he unfolded his plan to her. Good heavens, it was a devilish deception. It was almost cruel. Catherine would probably be furious. But he was determined to go through with it.

"This could be a tricky business," she said. "I am somehow supposed to ensure that no one addresses you as 'Your Grace.' How am I to do that, I ask you?"

"I shall leave it to you, Mother. The staff should be easy enough to control. They are used to my odd behavior."

"Well, I thank goodness you have always been such an eccentric, Stephen. I will have to use that reputation to warn the other guests not to acknowledge your position. Some of them think you are a loose screw anyway. This should put an end to any doubts on that score."

Stephen laughed again. "Isn't it delicious? Catherine herself told me the Duke of Carlisle was well known to be a half-wit."

"And Hetty tells me they believe we keep you locked up," she said, chuckling at the recollection. "Like the poor old King."

Stephen gave a bark of laughter. "Then you should have no trouble convincing them that I do not wish to be acknowledged as the duke. Just another of my dim-witted notions."

"To give you the benefit of the doubt, I will merely say it is simply another manifestation of your eccentricity. But you are Carlisle and we must all do as you say."

"Indeed."

"How does it feel," the duchess asked, "to have all the world think you crazy as a loon?"

"I could care less about all the world," he said, "but I have never felt happier in my life, Mother. And I am crazy, you know. Crazy in love with Catherine. And it feels wonderful."

"She will murder you when she finds out, you know."

"I know," he said with a wicked gleam in his eye.

"But then she will marry me and it will all have been worth it."

"You are indeed crazy, you know. I hope to heaven this lunatic plan of yours works."

"So do I, Mother. So do I."

Chapter 19

Catherine had the breath nearly squeezed clean out of her when she announced her plans to Susannah and Aunt Hetty the next morning. Their excitement filled Catherine's bedchamber, where she had gathered them to tell her news. Her aunt looked decidedly smug, as though she had actually had something to do with it all. Or as though she had known all along that Catherine would end up marrying for love rather than for a fortune. But then, Aunt Hetty was a hopeless romantic who never gave a moment's consideration to money, as Catherine knew well from experience.

Susannah was simply agog with excitement. "I knew it!" she squealed. "I just knew it! I knew you would not marry the earl for all the wrong reasons."

"I am afraid I disgraced myself terribly with Lord Strickland," Catherine said, blushing with shame at the recollection of his offer and her watery response. "I am sure I embarrassed the poor man to death. But he was so kind. And so understanding. I hope one day he finds someone who can really love him."

"I am sure he will, my dear," Aunt Hetty said. "And I am also sure he would never reveal to anyone

what took place between you. He is too much of a
gentleman to carry such tales."

"He is a very nice man, I am sure," Susannah said,
"but, just the same, I am glad that you refused him,
Cath. It would not have been right. But, my goodness,
I had no idea about Mr. Archibald! Why did you not
tell us, you sly goose?"

"I suppose I never really thought I'd have the nerve
to reject a fortune," Catherine said. "So there was no
point in mentioning him."

"I am so proud of you, Cath!" Susannah hugged
her for perhaps the hundredth time. Her ribs really
were becoming quite sore from all this enthusiasm.
Not to mention all the passionate crushing done by
Stephen the night before, she thought with a self-conscious smile. "And happy for you, too," Susannah
continued. "If you love your Mr. Archibald even half
as much as I love Roger, then I know everything will
be all right."

"And I owe it all to you, Sukey," Catherine said.
"Your wise counsel helped me to decide what to do.
Or scared me into doing it, I am not sure which. But
you could not have been more right. I cannot imagine
now that I almost turned my back on this happiness. I
have never felt this free in all my life."

"Free?" Aunt Hetty asked. "Free of what, dear?"

"Oh, I do not know exactly," Catherine replied.
"Free of worry, I suppose. Free of the burden to protect us all, no matter what. Free of my compulsion to
seek a fortune. Free to follow my heart. Oh, but, Aunt
Hetty, I am not completely free of worry. I still worry
about you. With Susannah and me both here at Chissingworth, what will you do? Will you keep the house
in Chelsea?"

"No, I do not think I will. As it happens, I have had
something of an offer myself," she said with a sly
grin.

"Aunt Hetty!" both sisters shrieked in unison.

"Do you have a beau?"

"Are you going to be married?"

"Who is it?"

"Why did you not tell us?"

"When is the wedding?"

"It is Sir Quentin Lacey, is it not?"

"Is it Mr. Gilchrist?"

"Is it Sir Isaac Crisp?"

"No, it is Lord Holbrooke. I know it is Lord Holbrooke."

"No, no, and no!" Aunt Hetty said, waving her hands and laughing. "I am not to be married, you silly girls."

"But, you said you had an offer," Susannah said.

"Not an offer of marriage," Aunt Hetty said. "The duchess has asked me to stay on at Chissingworth as her companion."

"Oh, my goodness!" Susannah exclaimed. "Then we shall all three be living together, just as always."

"Why, yes, we will. I had not thought of that."

"Oh, Aunt Hetty," Catherine said, giving her aunt a quick hug. It seemed a morning for hugs and kisses. "I am so pleased. I hated to think of you returning to Flood Street all alone."

"And I shall be here to watch both of you with your young men. And to see your children as well, when they come along."

Both sisters glanced at each other and blushed.

"What a wonderful day this is for us all," Aunt Hetty said. "And tonight, a ball to top it off."

"That reminds me," Catherine said. "Since Stephen's position does not allow him to attend the ball, it would be best if our betrothal is kept quiet until after the party. It would not be right to make it known when he cannot be there to share in the good wishes." And, Catherine thought, it might be embarrassing to Lord Strickland to discover I had thrown him over for the head gardener.

"Do not worry, my dear," Aunt Hetty said. "We will say nothing. You will have our silent good wishes for now."

"And do not be surprised if you see me sneak away early," Catherine continued. "I promised Stephen to meet him in the gardens after the duke's announcement."

"The duke?" Aunt Hetty's eyebrows shot up under her cap. "The duke is coming to the ball?"

"That is what Stephen tells me," Catherine said. "To announce his own betrothal. But perhaps that is meant to be a secret."

"My, my, my," Aunt Hetty said, shaking her head and smiling. "This should be most interesting. Most interesting indeed."

"It seems everyone at Chissingworth is finding new happiness," Susannah said. "Even the poor mad duke. Isn't that nice?"

Something set Aunt Hetty off, and she began to giggle. Catherine had no idea what could possibly be so funny, but her aunt did not seem to be able to stop laughing. Catherine and Susannah looked on in helpless ignorance as the older woman laughed and laughed until tears ran down her cheeks. Their aunt's mirth was infectious, and soon all three ladies were giggling over Catherine knew not what. Aunt Hetty finally gestured that she had to leave. Her hands fluttered in farewell as she opened the bedchamber door and stepped out into the hall. When she had closed the door, they heard one great shriek of laughter and then the sound of giggles slowly fading away as she must have walked down the corridor.

"Now what do you suppose that was all about?" Catherine asked.

"I have no idea," Susannah said. "But she is acting very queer, don't you think?"

The two sisters commiserated over their aunt's behavior, and then, after more hugs and kisses, parted for the morning.

Most of the female guests would be spending the day preparing for that evening's ball. The Forsythe sisters were no different. There were leisurely baths to take, freshly washed hair that needed drying, and last-minute additions of trim and such to ball gowns.

Catherine took special care with her toilette because she wanted to look nice for Stephen when they danced in the garden. Her dress was composed of a blush pink embroidered crepe robe. The embroidery was delicate and distinctive, and Catherine hoped Lady Fairchild would not recognize it. The dress itself had been completely transformed. Susannah had decorated the hem with a deep Vandyke fringe salvaged from one of their mother's old dresses. The wrist-length sleeves had been cropped and gathered into a short melon sleeve. The bodice had been raised slightly and the back lowered to echo the scoop of the neckline. A pink satin underdress had been provided by another old dress of their mother's. Catherine was very pleased with the overall effect, which was very soft and feminine. She felt pretty enough to celebrate her betrothal, even in the privacy of the garden.

Just before dinner, Molly arrived with a beautiful nosegay of pink violets. The accompanying note said only "I love you," and was signed with a big, scrawling "S." Catherine held the note to her breast for some minutes, thinking she might burst into tears once again. But the little maid, excited to be preparing her ladies for a ball, was too exuberant to allow Catherine a moment of sentimental reflection. She fussed over the flowers, trying them first in Catherine's hair, then deciding they should be pinned to the bodice. She made a few last-minute adjustments to the coiffure and announced herself satisfied.

"You and Miss Susannah will be the prettiest girls at the ball," she said, beaming with pride.

Catherine had not worn any more jewelry since her encounter with Lady Gatskyll. But this was a ball, after all. One had to wear something. She discarded anything with gemstones that might be recognized, as well as pearls with a distinctive clasp. She settled on a simple gold chain with an engraved locket. She folded Stephen's note into a tiny square and placed it in the locket. With both his flowers and his note close to her heart, she felt ready to face the world.

Dinner seemed endless, so impatient was she to get on with the evening. She was seated next to Sir Bertram, whose garrulous manner did much to disguise the fact that she said very little. Her eyes darted a few times toward Lord Strickland at the other end of the table. He caught her glance once and smiled warmly, and Catherine breathed a little easier. She had been worried that he might be embarrassed, but he did not seem to be so.

Catherine supposed it was she who ought to be embarrassed. The earl had not been the one to make a complete fool of himself. He was not the one who had become an uncontrollable watering pot. But she could not bring herself to be embarrassed. She was too relieved and too happy to feel bad about anything.

After dinner, Sir Bertram escorted her into the ballroom, where scores of other guests from the neighborhood had joined the party. There was no formal receiving line, since the duchess was the sole hostess. But she dashed about making each guest feel welcome.

The musicians began warming up for the first set, and gentlemen scurried here and there to secure partners. Since Catherine had already pledged the first set to Lord Warburton, Sir Bertram exacted a promise for a later set and took himself off to find a partner for the opening minuet.

Lord Warburton led her onto the dance floor and presented her with a very elegant leg while she curt-

sied to him. They circled and separated and came together again in the slow, formal movements of the old
French dance. Catherine had to bite back a smile as
her young partner struck a dramatic pose with each
pause in the mincing steps, as he exaggerated each
point of the toe and tilt of the head. It was a dance just
made for the foppish young lord and Catherine became quite caught up in the ridiculous artificiality of
it.

The minuet was incongruously followed by a lively
Scottish reel in which Catherine was partnered by Mr.
Brooke. She was quite enjoying herself, for she had
never before attended a real ball. Even so, her
thoughts often strayed to Stephen, hoping she would
soon be able to make her escape and join him in the
garden.

Lord Strickland claimed her for the quadrille.
Catherine was pleased, for she had worried that he
might ignore her. She really was quite fond of him, as
she had discovered the night before when he had
been so understanding and so kind. She would hate
for him to think ill of her. She smiled as he bowed
over her hand.

"You seem in much better spirits this evening, Miss
Forsythe," he said.

"Indeed, my lord," she said, her cheeks flushed
with embarrassment once again over her behavior last
night.

"Might I assume that your good spirits have something to do with that other gentleman you mentioned?" he asked.

Catherine's cheeks flamed even hotter at his question. How must she respond? How could she admit to
having rejected him one minute, and accepted the
offer of "that other gentleman" the next? The steps
separated them briefly, but as they faced each other
once again, his raised brows begged a response.

"Yes, my lord," she said softly, unable to meet his eyes. "You are quite correct."

"Then, I take it that situation has been satisfactorily resolved?" he asked.

Surprised that he would continue to pursue this topic, she looked up at him. "Yes," she said as she crossed the square of dancers to bow and twirl with one of the other gentlemen. She wished Lord Strickland would drop the subject altogether, for she really was beginning to feel rather uncomfortable.

When she returned to his side, he looked down at her and smiled warmly. "Then, let me be among the first to wish you happy," he said as they crossed hands and stepped in a circle with the other three couples. "I am very pleased for you, Miss Forsythe. You deserve all the happiness and good fortune he will bring you."

She darted a glance at him as he swung her around behind him. There appeared to be a distinct twinkle in his eye. Did he know about Stephen? That he was the estate gardener? And was he making a kind of teasing reference to Stephen's lack of fortune? And the fact that she had thrown away the chance to share his own fortune? Was there contempt behind that smile?

The steps took them apart again for some minutes and she was swung around by each of the other gentlemen before finally returning to face the earl. "You must be very pleased with how things have been settled," he said, grinning in an almost mischievous manner she would never have expected of him. And what did he mean by that remark? "To find yourself so well situated, after all," he continued.

He knew! He must know. Well situated, indeed. He knew she had betrothed herself to the gardener and was making fun of her. So, he was not so complacent about her refusal as she had believed. He was making it clear what he thought of being thrown over for a mere gardener. Catherine's cheeks burned with shame and outrage that he should say such things to her. She kept her jaw clenched and her chin high throughout the remaining movements of the quadrille, but said not a word to the earl. How dare he tease her about Stephen. How dare he presume that he was a better catch just because of his title and fortune. When the music stopped, she made the obligatory curtsy to the hateful man and turned to walk away. She spied Aunt Hetty seated along the opposite wall with Lady Malmsbury and headed in their direction.

And suddenly, the din of conversation throughout the entire ballroom came to an abrupt halt. What had happened? Catherine wondered as she looked around the room. It must be something very horrible or very momentous, for the silence was deafening. It then occurred to her that the duke must have arrived, for she could think of nothing else, short of an appearance by the Prince Regent, that could so thoroughly silence such a gathering. She sincerely hoped it was the duke, for then she could soon make her escape.

She followed the general gaze and movement of the crowd, and her eyes fell upon Stephen, strolling blithely into the ballroom.

What on earth? Stephen!

She stared at him, dumbfounded, as he walked toward her. She had only ever seen him in casual work clothes, comfortable and informal and usually rumpled. But she was dazzled just now by the sight of him in evening dress, and could not take her eyes off him as he moved through the room. He looked magnificent in a dark green velvet coat and white satin waistcoat embroidered with green and gilt. His hair was combed off his face. She wondered how long it would be before that one errant curl dipped over his brow. Good heavens, but he was gorgeous. Catherine experienced a sudden burst of pride that this beautiful man was to be her husband. He looked as elegant as a prince and walked as proudly. And he gazed straight into her eyes as he approached.

But what was he doing here?

He should not have come. He was not supposed to be here. Catherine noted people whispering and gawking as he approached. Good Lord, he was going to make a spectacle of himself. And of her, for he was so obviously headed straight for her. The crowd seemed to part at his approach, as if he were some sort of dangerous or repulsive creature. As if they wanted nothing to do with him.

Oh, Stephen! What ever possessed you to come? Why are you doing this?

He reached her side and smiled. Good Lord, he looked so splendid she almost forgot what a spectacle he was making of them both.

"Will you take my arm, Catherine?"

He did not give her a chance to reply, but took her hand and placed it on his arm. He turned her toward the orchestra dais where the duchess now stood, wearing a huge smile.

"Stephen!" she hissed. "What are you doing?"

"Trust me, my love," he whispered. "It will be all right."

But it was not all right. The entire ballroom stared at them. What was he doing? Why was he embarrassing her like this? She looked up to see the duchess still smiling and was more confused than ever. Surely Stephen must have been a valued family retainer for a long time. But she could not imagine *that* gave him the right to walk so boldly into his employer's ball, uninvited. And yet, he continued to lead her straight toward the duchess.

Catherine felt a hundred pairs of eyes on her and wanted nothing more than to escape. She tried to wrench her arm away, but he held it firmly in place and smiled down at her.

She had not thought it could get any worse, but

then he led her onto the dais. She stood there before the entire ballroom and was mortified. The duchess raised her hands for quiet, as if it were not already uncomfortably silent, and Catherine suddenly realized what was happening.

The duchess was going to announce her betrothal to Stephen. The way she grinned and beamed at both of them, it was obvious that was what she was about to do. The gentleman gardener—for he was surely a gentleman—must indeed be a valued retainer if the duchess condescended to make such an announcement.

Such a notion pleased Catherine. Perhaps he was not so lowly as she had believed. He looked anything but lowly this evening. Even so, she was thoroughly embarrassed and wished this were not happening. She recalled the earl's spiteful teasing and wondered what the others' reactions would be. Not really wanting to know just at that moment, she kept her gaze skewered to the floor.

She wished the duchess would simply get on with it, for Catherine was feeling flushed and warm and did not know how much longer she could maintain her composure.

Chapter 20

Stephen was perversely enjoying Catherine's dismay. He did not know what it was about her that provoked him to such deviltry. But ever since he had tripped over her in the garden, some imp of mischief had urged him into all sorts of badness. There was no excuse for it, except that he could not remember when he had had so much fun.

But just now, she must think him the worst sort of bounder, to drag her up on the dais with the duchess, every eye in the ballroom directed at them. He could feel her fingers trembling slightly where they rested on his arm. Poor thing. She was embarrassed. Stephen grinned and laid his hand over hers. She jerked her gaze from the floor and looked up at him. He gave her a look that he hoped told her all would be well. Her response was to stare daggers at him. Stephen grinned.

Good Lord, but she was angry. For some reason, that only increased his amusement. He could not wait to watch her mouth drop open when she figured out who he was. If he was not careful, he would soon be giggling like a fool. His reputation as the mad duke would be secure.

He composed himself, lifted his chin, and waited for his mother to speak.

"My dear friends," she began. Stephen noticed Catherine's gaze had dropped once again to her feet, and a deep blush colored her cheeks. She no doubt wished a chasm would open in the ballroom floor and swallow her up. Good Lord, she looked like she wanted to die. Stephen had only a moment to consider that this might not have been such a good idea, after all.

"I am so pleased," his mother continued, "that you are all able to join us tonight at our annual summer ball. Of all the balls we have held over the years here at Chissingworth, this one is the most special to me. For tonight I have the greatest pleasure to announce to you the betrothal of my son, Stephen, His Grace the Duke of Carlisle, to Miss Catherine Forsythe."

Stephen's wicked amusement was eclipsed by a moment of sheer pride and profound joy. He loved this woman and wanted all the world to know it. He beamed down at Catherine while gasps of surprise and delight floated up from the crowd.

She lifted her head ever so slowly and glared at him with huge eyes in a look of positive horror. Her dark brows crept up toward her hairline, and her mouth hung open, slack with astonishment. Stephen smiled down at her in reassurance. But she only stared at him with those big gray eyes. And suddenly, those eyes rolled up, her head fell back limp upon her neck, and she collapsed in a swoon at his feet.

"Catherine, my darling, are you all right?"

Her eyes fluttered open and she felt momentarily disoriented. What had happened? Stephen, in all his evening finery, bent over her with concerned eyes. She felt his arm around her shoulder and sank gratefully against it as she allowed her head to clear. She looked up to see her aunt and Susannah hovering nearby, and the duchess shooing away a crowd of curious onlookers.

"She will be fine," the duchess said. "She was merely overcome by the heat of the room. Please stand back and give her room to breathe."

And then she remembered.

Oh, my God. Stephen was the duke. The man she loved, the man she believed to be the head gardener was in fact the duke. The owner of Chissingworth. It was incredible. It was bizarre. It made no sense. But it had to be true. The duchess had called him her son and announced their betrothal to all the world. Good Lord, the man she had agreed to marry was the Duke of Carlisle.

She wanted to wring his aristocratic neck.

"You blackguard!" she whispered.

Stephen cocked a brow and grinned. He lifted her so that she was sitting upright.

"Why did you not tell me?" she said, keeping her voice low even though she wanted to scream at him. She had no wish to cause any more of a scene. Good Lord, she had actually fainted up on that dais, in front of the whole assembly. How thoroughly mortifying.

Stephen gently helped her to her feet and into a nearby chair. He pulled up another chair and sat beside her. Someone handed him a glass, and he put it in her hand. He kept his own hand around hers to steady the glass.

"Drink this," he said. "It is only water."

She obeyed him and took a swallow.

"Do you feel better, my love?" he asked. "Would you like to go to your room and lie down?"

She felt fine, but only glared at him and said nothing. How could he have done this to her. Good Lord, he was actually the duke? He looked every inch the duke in all his elegance. How had she failed to recognize the nobility beneath the rumpled exterior? When she thought of all she had said to him, thinking he was plain Mr. Archibald, she wanted to die. She had actually told a duke, an honest-to-God duke, that he was stupid and ignorant and she would have him fired. She winced as she recalled telling him that she had no interest in the half-witted Duke of Carlisle. Good Lord, what must he have thought of her? But she had also told him she loved him. She was not sure which was the more embarrassing.

"Why did you let me believe you were only the gardener?" she said.

"They *are* my gardens, you know."

Catherine suddenly became aware of all the concerned faces watching her and realized she did not want to have this conversation in public.

"I think I could use some fresh air," she said. "Would you walk with me in the gardens, Your Grace?"

"Only if you promise to call me Stephen again."

He put his arm around her shoulders as he led her from the ballroom, fending good wishes and congratulations along the way. He led her down the Great Stairway, along the main corridor, through endless salons, onto the terrace, and down the steps into the gardens—all without a single word.

Catherine used the silence to consider the situation. It occurred to her that Aunt Hetty must have known all along. She and the duchess were very close. And that unexplained laughter that morning must mean that her aunt had known. And Lord Strickland. He was not teasing her because she had refused him. He had known. The duke was his friend, as he had often said, so of course he had known. And he must have known that she did not know.

Good heavens, was she the last one to find out that she was betrothed to a duke? Did Susannah know as well? Had there been some kind of conspiracy to hide Stephen's identity from her? So that she would have to admit to the ignominy of falling in love with a mere gardener? So that she would be forced to examine more closely the priorities in her life? So that she would have to choose between love and money?

When she considered how near she had come to making the wrong choice, Catherine shuddered with remorse and shame.

Stephen kept his arm tight around her shoulders as they walked. Catherine gradually leaned closer into him, relishing the familiar comfort of his closeness. He led her silently through the formal grounds until they had reached the privacy of the Old Hall garden.

It was only then that he spoke. "I'm so sorry, Catherine," he said as he pulled her into his arms.

"Why did you not tell me?" she asked, burrowing her head against his shoulder. He may be the duke, but he still felt like Stephen, all warm and comfortable and with this one spot designed perfectly to fit her head.

"I wanted to know that you loved *me* and not . . ."

She lifted her head. "And not your fortune?"

He nodded and she pulled him closer and nuzzled his shoulder once again. She should have been furious. She should have been giving him a piece of her mind for putting her through such turmoil. And she should have been scared to death at the very notion of marrying a duke. Good heavens, she was to be a duchess! She had wanted a fortune, but she had never dreamed of reaching so high. But since she had admitted her love for Stephen, none of that seemed important anymore. She really should be thrilled at the prospect of the Carlisle fortune. But she was even more thrilled to be able to share it with Stephen. So what if he happened to be the duke?

"I do love you, Stephen," she said, raining soft kisses upon his face. "I'd like to murder you for what you just did to me in the ballroom." She kissed his jaw. "And I may never forgive you for letting me think you were nothing more than the gardener." She kissed his throat. "And I have every intention of exacting revenge for such infamous treatment." She kissed his eyes. "But I do love you. Oh, yes, Your Grace. I do love you."

And when she kissed his lips, he crushed her against him in a fierce embrace. She gave up a faint sigh of exquisite pleasure and opened her mouth to his.

After a long and passionate interlude, during which they each whispered words of love and apology and understanding, Stephen pulled Catherine to her feet and twirled her joyfully in his arms.

"Did I not promise you we would celebrate our betrothal by dancing here under the stars?" he asked.

"Hm," she murmured. Her cheek rested against his chest as he spun her around the garden in a shockingly intimate version of the waltz.

"I will always keep my promises to you, Catherine. I told you, did I not, that we would live happily forever here, together in this garden paradise?"

"Hm."

"I intend for us to do just that, my love. Even if I have to build a one-room cottage for us to live in."

And they laughed and twirled in their waltz beneath the stars, each having discovered a fortune in the other's arms.